THE ROOKIE AND
THE THIEF

Collected Stories 2010-2021

By Garbhán Downey

Colmcille
Press

December '21

To Bridget 7 Roger

Thank you

Garbhán

PREFACE

Street veteran-turned-statesman 'Harry the Hurler' Hurley believes the North's new politics will never work until they sort out
the police and the judiciary first.
But his Derry heartland is still reluctant to trust the old enemies.
So he takes two of his brightest young stars, convinces one to
join the PSNI and makes the other a lawyer.
The only problem is the would-be cop is an inveterate gambler,
while the soon-to-be judge is an incurable thief. And before long
they're on a collision course that not even Harry with all his buried ammo can prevent.
Packed with the edgy comedy, murder and mayhem which has
graced Garbhan Downey's previous works of fiction, The Rookie
and the Thief casts a satirical eye over the North's never-quite-
successful attempts to heal itself.
From the author of the critically-acclaimed short story collection Off Broadway: 'A master stylist, dammit, you can almost
taste the steam off the pages.' (Modern Woman)

I gcuimhne ar Áine, le grá

Even thieves have their own laws

MARCUS TULLIUS CICERO, D. 43 BC

FOREWORD

This book is in three parts. The main bit is a collection of a dozen interwoven short stories, focusing on the trials and triumphs of an young Derry power couple, one a cop the other a lawyer (The Rookie and The Thief). That's followed by a long short, Letters from Dublin, written in 2010 as a postscript to the novel The American Envoy. And we finish off with The Christmas Present, a limited-edition novella first published in 2016, which warrants a fuller airing.

This collection will appear in printed form with assorted nips and tucks later in the year. But it was a goal to have it on Colmcille Press's new eBook shelf before the summer. And we've just about made it.

Enjoy!

Garbhán Downey

www.colmcillepress.com

CONTENTS

THE ROOKIE AND THE THIEF

The Rookie and the Thief

H arry Hurley, the MP for North Derry, loves open spaces - they make for private business. And on a clear winter morning, there are few places more open and yet secluded to visit than the hillside cemetery. You can see for miles; down past the soccer stadium to the meandering Foyle; or across to the old walled city; or outwards to the frosted green hills of Donegal. And no-one, but no-one, can get within a thousand feet of you with a directional mike. Even when you're just swapping yarns.

"Back in the eighties," says Harry, stooping to replace a wind-blown wreath at the Republican plot, "there's this crowd of smarty-pantses who travel around the North from town to town, cleaning out the poker machines.

"It's a very simple little dodge – and there's nothing we can do about them, except keep our eyes sharpened and hide a big bat under the counter. What they do is they get tuppenny pieces and bulk them out using sticky tape until they're the same size as 50 pences. And when the arcade manager, or barman, isn't looking, they fill the machine full of these dud coins – and start shouting 'payout' as soon as they rack up a hundred quid in credit."

Harry's companion Dominic Dunne who, despite his tender years, has a three-year chip from Gamblers Anonymous, chuckles softly – both in appreciation of the dodge and to let his uncle know to go on.

"This particular week, the guys start closing in on Derry. Two of our pubs out in Dunavady are hit – but we only find out long afterwards, when we empty the machines at the end of the night. So we reckon they're going to try their hand in the city next. Probably Sparkly Barkley's big arcade on Hume Square.

"It's such a massive place that there's no way we can watch every machine twenty-four seven. There must be two hundred of them. And that's long before we've all the CCTV cameras, like we do now. So, how do we catch them...?"

Harry pauses, waiting for an answer. He looks hard at his companion, wondering if he's got the right man.

Dominic bites his lip and makes as if he's thinking. Truth is, though, this stuff is shelling peas to him. So he gives it a couple of minutes to please his uncle before replying.

"You make certain that no-one can win any more than say a score, or perhaps thirty quid, by rigging all the machines. It's nothing you're not doing anyway. Though maybe not so blatantly. So when the guy with the Belfast accent announces he has a full ton up, you quietly escort him to the back of the building to collect his cheque then bean him with a pipe."

Harry beams proudly. "I've nothing left to teach you, Dom. You truly are your father's son. And that's why I am so happy that you are going to join the police for me...

He takes a beat. "Though I must point out for the sake of accuracy, that we're a lot more subtle in our retribution than you give us credit for. Most of the time, there's no need for bodily violence. In this case, for example, Jimmy Fidget and two of our men simply wrap the little hood up in twenty rolls of masking tape, before heaving him into the river."

Dom laughs. "And people say you guys have no sense of irony."

"You're right," sighs Harry. "They have no appreciation of how hard we try..."

"So does the guy drown?"

"God, no. Not only do we give him a lifebelt, but we also wait until the dredger is passing. After all, it is only a first offence."

*

Dominic isn't really Harry's nephew at all. Rather, he is the son of Harry's cousin Dom Senior, who is lying this long time in the grave they are visiting. Back more than twenty years ago, when Dom Junior is only a toddler, his father is out on an errand for Harry when the car he is in blows up prematurely. And ever since, Harry treats the boy like his own son and heir. Better even. There are strong suggestions that the Brits are to blame for messing with the radio frequency that Dom Senior plans to use to detonate his bomb. But both Harry and young Dominic know it is pointless to reheat dead ashes. There comes a point when everyone has to move on. It's either that or you just get to live out the worst day of your life again and again and again.

There's always a mark left though – and in young Dominic's case, it's gambling. Cards, specifically. It's his other lasting legacy from his dead father. And up till three years ago, when he crashes out of law school under a cloud, Dom has a chronic problem.

It all starts when he's at school in Derry, and he's a lot cleverer than most of the guys he is making bets with. It's too easy for him, and before he goes to Oxford he's always two pages ahead. Harry does nothing to stop him, though – he needs his protégé to get it out of his system early. But at university, Dom is all of a sudden playing Texas Hold 'Em with guys who winter in Vegas and summer in Monte Carlo. And within a couple of years he is in serious trouble. And that's before he starts chasing his lost money.

"I still don't understand why it has to be me," Dom tells Harry, as they amble towards the cemetery bench. "As you're always saying yourself, I'm far too bright to be a cop. And now I finally have the bar exams, I can help you almost anywhere in the businesses. "Don't be coy with me, Dom. You know fine well why I want you there. With your brains, you'll be chief inspector in five years and running the city in seven."

"There's no guarantee I'll be posted here – knowing my luck I'll wind up in Newtownards or, Christ help us, Portadown..."

Harry shakes his head. "Are you making fun of me?"

They both laugh out loud. Harry has four seats on the Policing Board and a strangle-hold of politicos in the new Justice ministry. The only reason he doesn't appoint Dom to the top job directly is that he has to give the appearance of decorum. That, and he wants Dom to learn the trade.

"I still don't get why it has to be me though?" Dom presses.

"Don't give me that, Dominic," tuts Harry. "You know very well. There are three good reasons it's you. First, with Audrey out of the picture, I need my own eyes and ears in there. Someone with their wits about them; that I can rely on."

Audrey Grafton is Harry's second and final wife – and Derry's first ever female police superintendent, up until their wedding six months ago. It is no coincidence that she announces her transfer to the Southern cops on her step out the door to their honeymoon. Shacking up with the former Chief Executive of The Boys Inc does little for a girl's career prospects in the Northern Territories. Even now.

"Second," continues Harry, "we need to show we're serious about our support for policing. And what better way than for the son of one of our fallen brave to sign up and lead the way? 'If it's good enough for him, it's good enough for me...' Plus, you're an Irish speaker, you've two National League medals for Gaelic football and you never try to hide your politics – not even when you're swapping spit with the landed gentry at Oxford. There aren't many toasts at the Christ Church high table that finish off, 'Now give us back our land, you stuck-up, robbing bandits, and get to hell out of our country!' Only from what I hear, 'bandits' and 'hell' aren't exactly the words on the tape."

Dom grins. Again, Harry is making a good point. For many years now, it is perfectly acceptable to be a Catholic in the Northern police – indeed, they encourage it greatly. It is another matter entirely to be a republican and live outside the Castle. And Dom will not now, and not ever, tip his cap to the Crown. Nor does Harry want him to. It's different with Audrey – it's her tradition. But Harry wants people of his own to stand up and say I have a right to police my community too.

"And finally," smiles Harry, "there is the clincher."

Dom nods knowingly. "The bet?"

"Per-sackly," says Harry. "Now, what do I always tell you about gambling…?"

*

Dom, to be fair, normally resists all attempts to get him back to the card table. But a couple of weeks ago, he is sitting playing computer solitaire in his empty new law office above the Jack Kennedy Inn, when Harry's other heir apparent, Roisin Gilmore, pops up for a chat.

Roisin, who's better known as 'Curly' on account of her wavy-blonde Kate Hudson hair, is the daughter of Harry's sister, Donna – and is Dominic's best friend from childhood.

Curly is about a year younger than him, as fresh and pretty as a summer day, and is totally his type except for the fact that she's a high-wire act, who honours her late father by only dating war-damaged cops.

She is currently managing the Kennedy restaurant downstairs, while she finishes college. But she is also, as Dom is after discovering from his forensic inspection of the books, stealing exactly ten cents from every dollar going through the dining-room cash-registers.

"Jeez, Curly," he tells her, "you're going to have to knock it on the head or I'll have to let him know. You're not even making an effort to hide it."

She wrinkles her button nose like she's considering it carefully then shakes her head in a soft no. "I don't think you will," she says, laughing eyes challenging him. "I'm his blood – way closer than you. He'll believe you, sure. But he'll never forgive you."

"He's paying you over the odds, as it is – and you've stacks of your own money. Your old da, Jack, must have half-a-million in the bank by the time the drink finally catches up on him."

She gives him a knowing wink. "Try doubling that. You're forgetting about the stuff over the border."

He throws up his hands in frustration. "So why take the risk then?"

"The same reason you play cards, handsome. For the rush. There's no buzz on earth beats walking out of the Kennedy with four dirty twenties wedged into your shoes and another couple padding out your Victoria Secrets bra."

Dom lets his eyes drop to her chest momentarily then reddens as she catches him. "I'll take your word on that. But what are you going to do when he catches you? And you know for certain fact he will."

"I can't wait. He'll put me where I should be – at Stormont."

"Thieving on a larger scale?"

"Per-sackly."

They both laugh at the Harry-ism. But she has a point. Roisin has a Masters in Political Science from Trinity and is wasting her life dealing dishes for low-rent tips. And while Northern politics, in essence, amounts to little more than administering the budget of a small US city, it can be a jumping off point for a decent career.

"You ever going to finish that doctorate?" he asks, big brother again. "'Way I hear it, you're a nailed-down cert, if you ever hand it in."

Curly is within about two months of posting her PhD thesis in Post-Conflict Conciliation before the thing with her last boyfriend.

"Not sure. Maybe. There's a few of them very annoyed about the picture. I might let it settle for a year or so. Typical of my luck, his father is a pal of the external examiner."

"So the examiner knows about the photo?"

"God yes – he has his own copy. As does my entire contacts list."

"Ah, you eejit…"

"No-one takes a swing at me, Dom. Not anyone. If I can grow up in the most dysfunctional family in Europe and no-one so much

THE ROOKIE AND THE THIEF

as puts a finger on me, I'm damned if I'm going to let a two-bit detective take a slap at my cheek and walk away without some guidance notes."

And no-one is apt to forget any one of Curly's guidance notes. Her last boyfriend – a DC from Belfast – will never lift his hand to a woman again. For not only does Curly duck the slap and rabbit-punch him in his gentleman parts, but she then waits until he's out cold and dresses him up in her Ann Summers teddy and suspenders. And the same photo is a screen-saver on every police computer in the North, before Tommy 'Two Bottles' is finished with his hangover and returning his truncheon to its rightful position.

"So are you seeing anyone since?" he asks, averting his eyes from hers in case she might think he's asking for himself.

"Not at the minute. Word gets out fast – very few want to risk stopping over any more. What about you? You seeing anyone?"

Her eyes narrow a little. And it's more than curiosity. Unlike him, with his daft third-cousin rule, Curly is damn sure going to find out where this goes some day.

He gives her nothing. "You know my problem, Curly. Same as always - I can never see past you..."

She takes it on the chin, and then decides to shoot one back. "One of these days you're going to say that, and it's going to be true."

It lands and he lowers his eyes. None of the others match up. His many, many others. They don't challenge him like she does. But mostly because he doesn't want them to.

"Here," he interrupts, shaking his head clear. "Back to my point. Give me one good reason not to rat you out to Harry. You know what he does to the last guy who steals from him?"

"Yeah, but if he tries to tattoo my wrist with one of his 'I steal cars' logos, I'll show a few people where his bodies are buried. And I'm not talking figuratively either."

"You're putting me in a terrible bind here, Curly. He knows something's wrong. And if I turn up nothing, he'll think I'm in on it."

"I'll do you a deal so...we both want the same thing, don't we?"

"Do we?"

"Sure we do – the next spot that opens up at Stormont and Harry's job as an MP whenever he retires. Or takes one in the temple for Mother Ireland."

"Such poetry ... but I'm listening."

"I have a proposal," she continues, flicking her eyebrows at him in challenge. "You name any card game you like, and we'll play it for one hour. Chips only – no money – so you don't have to run off crying to your sponsor again. The winner gets a free run at the politics..."

"And the loser?"

"Gets to be Harry's go-to guy in the police. He needs one now that Audrey's away. He's at me night and day to join – reckons between my father and my last couple of boyfriends I'm halfway there already..."

She pauses for effect. "So if I lose, I'll be out of harm's way and you'll never have to tell Harry anything."

Dom smirks and shoots her a wise-up look. "No chance. You'll never sign up. You hate the police like poisoned apples. Ever since your father gets the bounce for helping out Harry that one lousy time."

"I'll make it more interesting so. Whoever wins the game has to pay the loser a chit promising to do them any favour they ask. A once-in-a-lifetime deal – without any question or demur – at any stage they are asked in the future."

Dom shakes his head not interested. "So if I win, you ask me to marry you, and I'm hammered anyway?"

"Don't flatter yourself, Blue Eyes. You're not a cop yet."

He stops again. Truth is, the offer is exciting – enticing even. And he is doing nothing anyway apart from losing four games of Solitaire out of five to a pre-rigged computer. "So to recap..."

She grins widely, showing off a set of teeth that are white enough to play piano on. "If I lose, you get to see me join the cops and maybe ask you a favour - like never, ever tell Harry what I'm doing this last three months."

"Hmm."

"And if you lose, Dom, you get to become Harry's number one

consigliere in his new war department. And you'll still have a shot at the MP's seat after I disgrace myself and the family name up at Stormont."

"And..."

"And you get to ask me the favour of lifetime." She bats the teasing brown eyes at him again. "And who knows, I might even say yes."

He's hooked. And like always, he knows he hasn't got a prayer. "Okay so. It's five-card draw..."

*

Curly is a rubbish gambler. She's always been far too smart to waste time playing cards; indeed Dom is left wondering if she's taking the contest seriously at all.

With just ten minutes to go of their hour, Dom is completely in control, holding about 90 percent of the chips. Curly has no strategy other than open, check and fold. Never risks a bluff. He'll just see right through it anyway. His eyes miss nothing – flickers, tics, scratching, he can read them all.

There are maybe three hands left to go when she gets a pair of openers. Almost certainly aces. He can tell by the way she pulls the pair carefully to the side of her hand.

She discards, taps the table and he deals her out three. She stares at her new hand then looks at her stack. She has a pile of twenty red chips in front of her – and moves five of them into the centre of the table.

She's saying she pulled nothing. But his opening jacks are now three.

He covers her five red chips then throws in fourteen more one at a time. Watching her eyes as she realises he's squeezing her out. Humiliating her too – leaving her one solitary chip to play with. Game to the end, she throws in fourteen reds – and then with a rueful smile raises him one.

Time to end the game. Time for Stormont. Time for Curly to enter the real world. He throws in a single red chip – and with an arrogant flourish, pushes all the rest of his chips – green, blue, white and red - into the centre of the table.

"It's mine," he says. "I'm buying you out."

"I'm afraid you can't do that," she retorts, "I'm all in. And now – so are you. It's the house rules."

"What the hell…?"

"Check downstairs, if you like. You can't buy me out. You have to let me cover a single bet with a loan. It's in our gaming constitution."

"What gaming constitution?"

"The one I'm after writing six weeks ago…Would you like to see the book?…And I would now like to borrow from the bank exactly what I need to cover your bet – that is all your chips. Though, as you'll be aware, I can't raise you on a loan."

"No, of course you can't…"

He closes his eyes and shakes his head, trying not to laugh at his own stupidity.

She looks at him almost pityingly. "You want to see my cards now?"

"I don't need to. You have another ace, don't you?"

"Of course I do, handsome. And I'm afraid, as far as this game goes, you're out of business."

She flicks the three aces over casually, as if it is something she does every day. And this time he does laugh. "Well done. No matter how many times Harry warns me, I never hear him."

"What? About the cards?"

"No … about you."

This time she laughs. "Okay so. Now ask me your favour."

"I don't have to do it this minute, do I?"

"No. But I have to say, you'll be catching me in a pretty good mood…"

He nods graciously. "Okay, then. Roisin, I want you to go to Harry and tell him that you owe him eight thousand pounds from the restaurant, and that you are going to pay him back as soon as your father's estate is properly valued. You can tell him that I'm approving of your extra drawings all along - and that we now want to put them on the books."

She bites her lip angrily. "You dirty lowlife. No way. No way. No way. You're just doing this to get back at me."

"Then no deal on the other..."

He is playing her right back. Her pretty face is now puce, and for the first time there are brief shadows of doubt in her eyes. "You are one cold, cold-hearted man, Dominic. You'll do well in the police. And to think, I, I..."

"As do I, Roisin. But if we ever do hook up – and it's always possible - it'll not be because of a damn card game. You, me and us are far too damn important to my life to throw away on the turn of a card. Now, go and get your little speech ready for Harry – and let him know that he can lay off pushing you towards the cops; you're lining up another patsy for him."

She is still seething. No-one beats her like this. "I hate you more than you will ever know."

"And I love you more than you will ever know," he mutters back to the banging door.

*

Harry stretches his arms out over the back of the cemetery bench and takes in the misting view below. "So do you want to talk about this bet, then?"

"Not really. Other than to say, you're a rogue Uncle Harry – and it's very unfair of you to play with my head like that."

"I have no idea what you're talking about. Are you suggesting I'm behind this? How dare you."

But he can't keep it up and, as Dom slowly counts to twenty in his head, Harry's face cracks into a smirk.

"All right. All right. I give in. Where's the fault-line?"

Dom smiles back. Now he's sure. "The cards. She's obviously taking lessons from someone who knows a little but not a whole lot. And no offence, Harry, but you have only one trick."

"And what's that?"

"You kick for touch and kick for touch, like a novice, until you get a decent hand. Then as soon as you've the winners, you bet small like an amateur, so everyone rushes in to crush you. Then, the second they overreach themselves, you lean forward and cut their throats. You're doing it all your life – both on the table and off of it."

Harry nods wisely. His nephew reads people better even than him. But he's not sure he likes the dig. Very disrespectful. "One trick, ha? What about the five percent I get her to shave out of the till receipts – to get you all wired up."

"Five percent?" Dom grins. "You do know she's taking ten?"

Harry buries his head in his hands and starts to laugh. "You're kidding."

"Nope."

"Dammit. It's my own fault. Never teach anyone to steal."

"I won't."

"But it's also why I can never have her in the cops…"

"Why set her on me so?"

"You know the answer to that one – who else am I going to use on you, Dominic? And in fairness, you're a natural cop. You're like me – you miss nothing. Besides, I can't have you wasting your time up in Stormont; you're much better learning a real apprenticeship. Curly is young and needs a few edges knocked off her. Maybe I'll get her into the Banking Committee – keep them on their toes. Set a thief, and all that."

"You know there's a fatal flaw in your plan, though. With the cards, I mean."

"And what's that?"

"I know all along that Curly has the third ace."

"I don't believe you. How's that? Has she a tell?"

"About a dozen of them. But also, I'm dealing – and I know that her ace is lying right before the third jack I'm after pulling myself."

Harry smiles again. This time with real affection. "So, you're after throwing yourself in front of a car for me?"

"God no," replies Dominic with a soft sigh. "I'm after throwing myself in front of a car for Curly."

Ronnie the Redcoat's Rain Gear

It is Dom's turn to bring the sandwiches and the story. "When redcoats turn in their caps," he says, "there are generally only three other people at the retirement party..."

"I'm surprised there are so many," replies Harry, throwing his bespoke jacket over the wrought-iron coat stand at his office door. He quickly clears a bunch of Christmas cards from his seven-foot long desk, flops his middle-aged carcass down onto the soft leather chair and swings his brogues up onto the mahogany. He furrows his brow while he considers his nephew's opener. "I'll bite so. Why are there three?"

"Two are other redcoats there for the free beer, and the third is a guy with a grudge and a knife under his coat, who slips past security downstairs."

Harry laughs - but only because he knows it is true. There are few animals on the planet less loved than Derry's hard-pressed parking attendants. Indeed, to rework the old gag, if he is stuck in the same room with Simon Cowell, Cheryl Cole and Louis Walsh, and only two bullets, he will shoot the redcoat outside the window - twice.

"So what has you thinking about redcoats today?" he asks his nephew.

Dominic shrugs, as if embarrassed. "I'm after cracking my first big case – and am going to get a note on my record. The good type. And yes, it involves a redcoat. Though before you ask, unfortunately no, not the murdering, maiming or permanent disfiguring of one."

"In that case, I'm not interested."

"It involves a couple of parking fines we can't process."

"Bo-ring. What's the point of you training to be a detective, if you're going to spend all your life chasing bits of paper?"

"It is how we do it now. And while you're at it, why not ask Al Capone the same question? These days, you're more likely to be laid low by an accountant than a smoking gun."

Dom's voice is starting to get a little more serious and more than little antsy – but then he catches the mischievous glint in Harry's eye and pulls up short. He grins to acknowledge he is nearly after walking into his uncle's bear-trap.

Harry smiles back and nods well played to Dom. But he also knows that his nephew is not going to waste his time with a shaggy dog story. "All right, all right," he sighs, chomping deep into his turkey and cranberry bap, "tell me about these fines, so, Elliot Ness."

*

Dom tears a huge chunk out of his chicken tikka wrap and swallows about a quarter pint of milk to wash it down. "As you're aware, they don't want me near anything remotely controversial until they get a good look at me. They know I'm the son of a dead rebel, and – thanks to you sticking your oar in to get me posted to Derry for training, Harry – they also know who I am connected to. So for the minute, they won't even let me on the computers.

"The senior guys are polite enough – they're smart enough to realise I'll be passing them by some day. But a lot of the middle-rankers hate me – and make it clear that people like me, and indeed you, have no place in their police.

"So, I get to spend most of my time sitting in the little office behind the front desk, answering the phone to nosey busybodies and assorted headcases – or chatting to the redcoats who are allowed to use our locker-rooms. The redcoats are mostly decent to me. They're too far down the food chain to care about the politics of policing. All they worry about is hitting their targets and maybe scoring a bit of overtime to get the bedroom done up in time for Christmas.

"But boy are they ruthless when it comes to doling out dockets. They're not interested in excuses or apologies or whose mother is dying in the back seat. All they want to do is get the ticket under the wiper blade and stick another credit in the Win Column.

"There's fierce, fierce competition to be top dog – spurred on, of course, by the bonuses it can earn them. Every year there's a ten grand prize from management for the highest earner in each district."

Harry pulls a disgusted face. He despises all traffic cops and their redcoat cousins ever since he gets put off the road for turning the bag the wrong colour. "Shocking," he sniffs, "profiting out of our misery like that."

Dom nods sadly in agreement. It is speed with him – any more points on his licence and he'll get to spend the next year pedalling the seven miles out to Maydown Station on the company mountain-bike.

"Last year," says Dom, "the contest is a very close run thing in Derry between two of the top redcoat hitters – Dick the Devil and Ronnie Moulins."

"I remember Dick the Devil well – he's the guy that clamps poor Curly, the day she's outside the chemist getting her old man the morphine."

"Yup, that's the same guy. A perfect charmer. Though despite what the doctors are saying at the time, his testicle is starting to descend again and may even work again someday."

"So who's the other guy?"

"It's a girl actually. Veronica's her real name – but she gets Ronnie on account of, well, her boyish physique."

"Not so pretty, then?"

"On the contrary, from what I hear she's far too good looking for the job she's in. She has a face like an angel. But despite the fact she's only in her early thirties, she has this chronic arthritis, so she always wears wet weather gear and a sweater."

"Which makes her look like a dude."

"A little - certainly enough for the other redcoats to make fun of her. They even have a song about her – 'Ronnie the Redcoat's Rain Gear'…"

"Very clever. So I suppose she then spends her days taking it out on every poor innocent taxpayer who parks half an inch the wrong side of the tracks?"

Dom shakes his head. "Actually, no. Not even close. Ronnie's problem is that she's far too fair-minded, and ultimately it's why Dick the Devil is after picking up the ten grand cheque for being City Centre Pariah of the Year."

*

Fair-mindedness is not a complaint that is often levelled at red-coats. But ever since she starts in the trade, as a teenager back in Belfast ten years ago, Ronnie has a reputation for decency.

Her manager then is a hugely intelligent young computer buff, name of Johnny Sparks, who is only in the business after the university sacks him for using their machines to forge a couple of lousy concert tickets.

Unlike most of his ilk, Johnny does not believe in further persecuting cash-strapped drivers who spend twelve quid on a day-pass, only to have some jobsworth fine them another thirty because their slip isn't displayed properly on the dashboard. So Johnny instructs Ronnie, who he is a little sweet on, to remember the little guy – and always use her best discretion. Which she does.

Ever since she transfers to Derry, about five years back, Ronnie will never put a ticket on any car with a baby-chair or booster seats inside, even if it is sitting in the middle of the Mayor's Parade. She has ambitions to be a mother herself sometime and figures it will be an expensive hobby enough already.

Likewise, she tries hard never to ticket anyone over sixty years old, as they need all the spare change they can get to survive the Irish winters.

And, if a car is more than ten or twelve years old, it is a fair bet that its owner would be better off putting their £30 to a new set of tyres, than handing it to the neighbourhood Docketing and Clamping Authority. So they get a bye-ball too.

If however, you drive a Mercedes and leave it on a double yellow, you better hope you have at least the president of a small European country in the car, otherwise your front wheel will be locked up tighter than a pole-dancer's toy-press. For Ronnie has no time for big money throwing itself in her face.

Or indeed, if you are an 18-year-old boy-racer and park in a disabled zone, Ronnie will have your new alloy wheels minced up in the Maydown crusher, before you can even get your ten-dollar stash out of the glove compartment.

Despite the fact she's all weighted down with her weatherproofs, Ronnie moves like lightning around her patch. Even without the quarter of her clients that she roundly ignores, Ronnie still manages to equal the ticketing rate of even the very best. Except perhaps Dick the Devil – who, as you'll gather, gets his name due to the fact he has no discernible soul whatsoever.

It also helps that she has the biggest patch in the city – a full six-acres, taking in many of the busiest shopping streets. And better again, her route is mostly flat ground, a near impossibility in this mountainous city. This is a beef of contention with Dick, who complains loudly that the only reason she has the patch is that her old pal Johnny is still looking out for her, even after she dumps him back in Belfast for the sunny slopes of Derry. Though, Ronnie's friends - and somewhat surprisingly for a red-coat, she has many - point out that her arthritis doesn't do well on hills and that her new bosses are just trying to give her a fair shake.

Dick reckons he will double Ronnie's output if he ever gets a chance – and is constantly telling his superiors the same. So much so, they eventually listen to him and announce that the winner of this year's top ticketing prize will be allowed to have first pick of next year's patches.

This adds even more needle to the competition – and Ronnie steps it up a gear, as she is desperate to hold onto her route. She never compromises her principles, though – her three P's. No tickets for pushchairs, pensioners and the penniless.

Dick has no so qualms, however – indeed there is a near riot when he books four limousines for mounting the pavement outside Guildhall, despite the fact they are carrying a visiting trade delegation from New York. The Town Clerk is so angry that he rips up the tickets and apologises to the guests. But Dick then threatens to call the papers – pointing out that if he is ticketing guys who earn £100 a week, the same laws apply to the guys who earn a thousand times that. And he makes the Town Clerk write him a cheque for the tickets on the spot before he lowers his phone.

Unfortunately for Ronnie, Dick's tenacity is hard to match. She is further hampered by the fact that the prize is based on fines paid – that is, money in the jar – rather than simply tickets issued.

So on January 1, when the tallies are in, she is broken-hearted to learn that despite the fact she issues more dockets than Dick, he is after beating her by one solitary fine in returns – thirty lousy quid.

Dick is typically graceless in defeat and immediately demands Ronnie's old patch, suggesting that they allocate her the old Fountain Hill ski-lift route in return. But Ronnie knows her legs will never hack the daily climb, and quietly declares that she is going to retire.

It is a sad day for the city, losing a redcoat with such a good heart – particularly to make way for one as rotten as Dick the Devil. But life is full of sad days, and before long Ronnie is as forgotten and unlamented as the rest of yesterday's hard-luck stories. It is possible she returns to Belfast, but nobody is really sure.

*

"But then," says Dominic, ripping open his post-sandwich pudding, "three weeks ago, at the start of December, a very strange thing happens.

"I am sitting in the locker room about to change back into my street-duds, when Frank McElkelly, the redcoats' regional boss, comes in and hands me a letter addressed to him personally. In-

18

side it is a short note, and two cheques, each for thirty pounds. He asks me to see if I can find out what it's about – as he can make neither head nor tail of it..."

Harry quickly raises his finger to say hold that thought, then buzzes his intercom three times to tell his secretary they want their coffee. "I have it," he says triumphantly. "The cheques are on Ronnie's account. They can now be added to her total – and she will get her patch back, plus the ten-grand winner's cheque."

Dominic grins a little proudly and shakes his head. "Close. But so far away at the same time. The note, I will inform you, is from a very upright Christian, who says he is trying to pay his parking fine for almost a year now, as all righteous men must do. But he is very concerned that the Belfast address keeps returning his envelope."

"I don't understand," says Harry.

"And neither does McElkelly, which is why he asks me to follow it up. So I ring up the God-botherer to get his story. This guy apparently has a suspect back and twice has the bad luck to leave his Jaguar five minutes too long outside the chiropractor's. Ronnie nabs him both times, but he is a big boy, with a few quid, and knows he has no right to complain. But here is the crux. Since the start of this year, Mr Saved tries eight times to send in his two cheques - but each time the letter bounces back. Until about a month ago, he decides to send the cheques directly to the police station in Derry – where he knows McElkelly is based – in the hope that he will deal with the matter directly."

"Very gracious of him."

"So I quiz Mr Born-Again about the address he is trying originally – and sure enough it is the correct one, line by line. Until the post code – where he is out by one digit."

"Aha," laughs Harry, "I hear that can make all the difference."

"You don't know the half of it. This is by no means our man's first parking ticket, however. Between himself and his missus, they have a collection of about twenty dockets over the past five years. So much so, that the address for paying the fines is lodged in their computer. And they are paying the fines all the while to this same address with the wrong code – but these are the first two cheques ever to come back."

"Very curious," says Harry, puzzled.

"It gets better. McElkelly can't find the duplicates of the new tickets anywhere in the office – nor any processing reference to them. And this annoys him greatly, as he can't cash the cheques unless he can stamp the charge number on their backs. More importantly still, he hates Dick the Devil with a vengeance, and he wants to lord it over him that he is, and will always be, the number two redcoat in the city. Although, sadly, according the rules it is too late to take back the ten grand prize."

Dom stops briefly as Kylie comes in with the tray of coffee, performs a sarcastic little French maid curtsey and disappears out the door again. Harry casts his eyes upward ruefully: "She doesn't like being buzzed at. It's demeaning and disrespectful, yada, yada, yada. Anyhow, go on..."

His nephew grins. "This day last week, I have little to do in the office, so, just out curiosity, I decide to try and track down Ms Veronica Moulins aka Ronnie. Ridiculously, the redcoats don't have a Derry address for her. The last contact that personnel can find for her is back in Belfast and is at least six years old. So, I get that from them – and try ringing the number, but it is disconnected. So I am sitting looking at her old address, wondering what to try next – or to whether to ditch it in the TFB file..."

"TFB?"

"Yeah, the 'totally baffling' file. Then all of a sudden something strange hits me."

"What? That you're after wasting twenty years of an education and a ton of my money to go chasing after rainbows?"

"No. I notice that the post code in her last address is exactly the same as the post code that our Born Again friend is making out his parking tickets to for the past five years. So then..."

"–Then you decide to track down Johnny Sparks."

"Per-sackly. And Mr Sparks's last known address is...you're starting to get it, the same house again. So I dig a little deeper and get personnel to give me full files for both Ronnie and Johnny, and I discover that back when she's a trainee in Belfast, Ronnie actually loses her first ticketing machine – in a mugging. That's eleven years ago now."

"–Around about the same time that Ronnie and Johnny both register at their new address, by any chance?"

"Just three months before it. So I check their banks and discover that they have a joint account for a company they both own called 'Fines Processing Branch', which coincidentally is going these eleven years now, and which is registered solely to their post code address. Now, of course, no such similar department exists in the redcoats – or at least not by that title. But a punter who is making out a cheque for a legal docket that is only slightly altered by a master-forger is never going to know that..."

Harry claps his hands in delight. "Brilliant. And they're doing it how long?

"Ten years, until she retires last New Year. She doesn't have arthritis at all – at least that's what her doctor tells me – she just wears the wet weather gear day after day to hide the second machine that is strapped to her side."

"Awesome." Harry is beaming. "I love this woman. How much do you reckon they have?"

"I chatted to McElkelly and to his boss – and to Ronnie's banks, which as you'll expect are all cleaned out this long time – and we think it's somewhere in the region of two million five, maybe as high as three. Best we can tell, about half of all Ronnie's tickets over the decade are wrong ones."

"Wonderful – so are you going to go after them?"

"No. And here is the really beautiful part – we can't."

"Why not?"

"Well, if the redcoats announce that one of their number has been issuing invalid dockets, then there will be a stampede from here to Cullybackey of innocent citizens looking for their money back. And as you can imagine, neither the redcoat managers nor my own long-suffering bosses reckon that will do anything for civic harmony or their own coffers."

"And what of Johnny and Ronnie?"

"Spain, maybe? Australia? No idea. Johnny has the money so well hidden away, we'll never find it – or them."

"So they get to keep the lot?"

"That they do."

"And you get a stripe in your arm for working it out?"

"Well, my line managers are so pleased at me for spotting the loophole – and then having the sense not to talk about it that they are going to cut my probation time in half. But even that is not the best news of the day..."

"So what is?"

"Well just before lunchtime, McElkelly calls me aside to tell me that he is demoting Dick the Devil back to the Fountain Hill patch."

"Can he do that?"

"McElkelly can do what he wants."

"But how?"

"Well, he tells Dick that it is because the Town Clerk won't forgive him for the showdown last year with the limos and wants him out of the city centre. And Dick is around long enough to accept that this is how it goes – and that he has no option but to suck on this particular thistle. But privately, McElkelly confides in me that he has his own reason."

"Which is...?"

"Which is if Ronnie can steal half her takings and still bring home as much as Dick, then there is no way Dick is good enough for the prime spot."

"–So Dick is going to be walking up and down the ski-route, while Ronnie gets to spend Christmas sunning herself on some faraway beach?"

Dom nods happily. "Heart-warming, isn't it?"

"It is indeed," smiles Harry. "Thank you Dominic, for that uplifting Christmas message. There is justice in the world - even for redcoats. God bless us every one."

The Sleepover

Harry Hurley MP prefers to walk and talk. For two reasons. Firstly, owning his own restaurant is proving a disaster for his middle-aged bulk – and his new wife Audrey is damned if she is after giving up a career in the Northern police just for him to keel over and die on her. So, unless he gives his heart at least one proper workout during the day, he'll damn sure not be giving it another one at home.

Secondly, Harry reckons, rightly, that it is much, much harder for unwelcome interlopers to hear, or record, what he is saying, when he is outdoors and talking out the side of his mouth. So, every day, immediately after lunch, he pulls his Mercedes 500 out of the Kennedy Inn and heads off for wide-open-spaces unknown – unknown that is to everyone except Harry and his postprandial meet.

Within a fifteen-minute drive of his office, Harry has more than a hundred of the most picturesque walks in Ireland to choose from – depending on whether he is in the form for rivers, mountains, beaches, lakes, golf courses or historical cityscapes. Today, though, he wants to keep it close to home, and proposes a stroll along the Foyle embankment and across the new footbridge to St Columb's Park.

He pulls up in Sainsbury's carpark beside his nephew's sawn-off BMW, and the two men amble slowly across to the broad riverside walkway.

"What's this about?" asks Dominic, as they point themselves south towards the Guildhall. Dom knows that Harry will have a pretext for seeing him before he begins probing him about what's really going on inside Derry's biggest police station. Harry might have four of his guys on the new Policing Authority – and another couple of soldiers on the Justice Committee – but there is no substitute for the inside track.

"Just want to check up on those cash register discrepancies over the Christmas period," his uncle replies. "You get anywhere on it yet?"

"Oh yes, the great New Year rip-off," smiles Dom. "Twelve hundred of your hard-earned sobs missing in action. Yes, I have some news – but you're not going to like it..."

"Well, at least I know it's not Curly – now she's up at Stormont..."

"Since when? Doing what?"

"Couple of weeks now. We're breaking her in as Paddy O'Carthy's replacement."

"Oh, is Paddy retiring as an MLA?"

"Yes. In six weeks time. But keep it quiet. He doesn't know yet."

"Christ, and people think policing is dirty... Anyhow, back to my point. I have your thief."

"Who is it?"

"Your wife."

"What?"

"Yeah. Word reaches her ears that you are scrimping on the Christmas hospitality this year. Only one free drink per punter. My God, man, how much money do you need?"

Harry sniffs grumpily. "You give away your own money; leave me in charge of mine. So she's robbing me blind to teach me a lesson."

"Not at all. She instructs the staff to open a free bar between eight and nine on New Year's Eve – but not to mention it to you and to put it on your personal tab."

Harry winces – both at the thought that he's never seeing the money again and the embarrassment that Dominic is after working it all out. "I'm going to sack that hopeless, no-guts manager. Danny takes his orders from me and me alone."

"Really?" smirks Dom, knowing well Harry is just getting it out of his system.

"Well, at the very least I'm dragging him into the cool room and kick his arse."

"Very brave of you. In which case Danny says to inform you – and

by the way, in case you're wondering, Danny is indeed my mole for all of this – if you lay so much as a cashmere glove on him, he will run and tell teacher. And we all know how that one ends..."
Harry laughs out loud. "We do. With me being spanked – and not in a good way."
"Per-sackly," says Dom. "But look, just think about the amount of goodwill that you'll get when people hear you have the bar free for an hour. They'll be coming in from all four provinces to see if you ever do it again."
"Which I won't."
"Of course not. Just so long as you remember to keep Audrey tied up in the dungeon for the entire holidays."
"That I will...But how do you know about my dungeon?"

*

They walk past the restaurant plazas and around the marina, which is devoid of all but a couple of mid-winter tugboats.
It is, Harry reckons, time to rectify the balance of power. "So I take it you're not seeing much of Curly this weather?"
Dom gives him a sideways grin and nods as if by way of agreement. "Work commitments, you know yourself..."
"Way I hear it, she's doing a new line with your shift sergeant."
"Not my concern, Harry. And never will be."
"One of these days, Dominic, you're going to work out what the rest of us already know... All right so, I'm lying about your sergeant to get a rise out of you. But only because Curly is asking me to."
"You can tell her for me, that my sergeant is a six-foot-two, fifteen-stone body-builder, who is just perfect for her."
"What's his name so?"
"Amanda..."
They both snort.
"Actually, I'm a little disappointed in Curly," continues Dom. "We're chatting on the phone again pretty regularly – since our fight a while back. But it's the first I'm hearing of this new job."

"Yeah. As I say, we're still keeping it tight. By the way, be sure and hear it from someone else first... So what are you two talking about anyway?"

"Business, believe it or not. She needs a little help – or rather one of her pals does."

"Which pal?"

"Patsy Barkley, King Size's widow."

"Ah, the poor, innocent girl. Never going be your first pick for the quiz team, for all her money. You know to run away very quickly if she ever throws a pin at you?"

"Why's that?"

"She'll still have the grenade in her mouth..."

Dom rolls his eyes. "...Anyhow, as you quite rightly point out, Mrs Barkley can be an easy target for unscrupulous types, so when she makes a new pal in the form of a nurse who's on secondment from Dublin at Altnagelvin hospital – a very pretty young single mother called Sandy – Curly rings me up and asks me to do a background check on the new girl."

"Why's that?"

"Curly is like yourself Harry – she has great instincts about people. And she isn't happy at all that this Sandy seems to be taking advantage of Patsy's good nature – sticking her for dinners out, weekends away, the odd pair of shoes, that sort of thing. They both have children who are about ten. Patsy has a little son called Marky, who is her spitting image only very, very smart – and it is him who alerts Curly that all is not right. And Sandy has a dark and creepy little boy of the same age, called Hector – who Marky dubs 'Hector, Hector the Snotter Inspector' on account of his less-than-salubrious feeding habits."

"Yeah, but a coupla dinners and a pair of shoes – what's the harm in that? Maybe Curly's just worried Patsy's starting to ditch her for a prettier model."

"Which is exactly what I say to Curly. Whose reply, incidentally, is a popular seven-letter phrase containing three 'fs', and which you'll almost never find on *Jeopardy*. No, Curly believes, as does young Marky, that Sandy is merely waiting for a chance for the big kill."

"So is she?"

"That's only half of it."

*

Last week, says Dominic, Sandy is on overnight shifts, so after about a thousand subtle hints, Patsy agrees to host a sleepover for the two boys at her huge house on the riverbank. It saves Sandy a night's babysitting fees and also means she can have breakfast with her boyfriend, a young Casualty doctor trapped like a rabbit in her headlights. Sandy, like many of her ilk, has only one good trick, but she plays it well.

Young Marky protests strongly against Hector's visit. Besides his fondness for storing his dinner up his nose, Hector is also a complete snake. He steals toys and money, tells tales out of school, starts fights and then kisses up to the adults as soon as they enter the room. (He is, Dom reckons, absolutely destined for a career the law.) But Mother Patsy, who is a good and innocent soul, tells Marky it is important to be kind to those less fortunate than you – and to suck it up if he wants his new iPhone for Christmas.

The first part of the evening does not go well. The boys fight over everything from dinner menus to sleeping arrangements – "not in my room, not now, not ever" – to what DVD to watch before bed – "not fecking *Toy Story*". Hector, however, is always the guy caught with the wounded look on his face when Patsy busts in, and eventually, Marky is sent upstairs for an early bath.

"I'm going to sort you out later," he warns Hector.

Hector waits until Patsy's eyes are averted then discreetly offers Marky the middle finger.

Marky, who is generally quite level-headed, makes a dive past his mother for his nemesis, fists flying. "I'm going to kill you, Hector. I'm going to do you in."

But Patsy manages to get a decent grip on Marky's ear before he can do damage. "My apologies, Hector. Marky's normally a very good boy. But he's obviously not used to sharing. You stay here and watch the end of *Toy Story*, while I put him to bed."

Marky quickly realises he's not winning this round so storms up to his room, locking the door after him.

Patsy is worried, though – it's not like her little boy at all to be so fiery. So, after the DVD is over, instead of trying to slip Hector into the other bed in Marky's room, she takes her guest to a spare bedroom, hands him a mug of hot chocolate and wishes him a very good night.

Hector smiles a sweet thank-you and says he wishes to read for a while, if that's okay. Which, of course, it is.

Patsy then knocks gently on her son's door, hears the gentle snoring and heads quickly downstairs for a stiff Chardonnay while the going's good.

*

If the first part of Patsy's evening is less than perfect, however, it is about to take a sharp left turn for the worse. About ten minutes later, she is sitting channel-hopping in her living room, half a bottle down, when she hears an unmerciful roar from upstairs.

"Help!" goes the scream. "Help me! I'm being poisoned."

Patsy, who is, naturally, blessed with big long legs, takes the stairs three at a time and rushes into Hector's room. There, she sees her young guest, writhing on the bed in mortal agony.

"The cup," he cries. "The cup - there are pills at the bottom of the chocolate."

Sure enough, Patsy grabs the mug from the nightstand and can see four little white tablets dissolving like marshmallows in the last of cocoa.

"But how?"

Hector, who is very white now, gasps, "I don't know. But when I'm in the en-suite, there are some noises out here. It has to be Marky."

Patsy then looks in the waste-bin and sees an empty pill-bottle.

It's the Diazepam that Doc Clancy prescribes her after her late husband King Size is killed. But it turns out that she never needs them.

Forty high-dose sleeping tablets, maybe thirty-six of them now inside a small boy.

"Oh God, no. You have to stay awake, Hector. Don't worry. Look, we have to get you straight to hospital. I'm going to take you myself – and we'll ring your mother on the way."

"What about Marky?"

Patsy runs and bangs on her son's door. But she can hear the snores. She bangs again, louder, and eventually he unbolts the door and opens it, sleep clouding his eyes. "What?"

"We have to go to hospital. How many tablets are you after giving Hector?"

"What? None, Mammy. I'm just awake this second. Honest."

"Get into the car, you little liar. We're taking him to hospital. You're going to have to talk to the doctors."

Patsy helps Hector to her big gold Beamer and lies him across the back seat. He is in considerable pain, a rotten white colour and sweating very badly. "Stay awake, son. Don't worry. Just stay awake, and we'll pump them all out of you."

Marky gets into the front beside his mother and doesn't say a word.

Four crashed red lights later, and Patsy tears into the Emergency carpark, where Sandy and her beau, Doctor Lovebucket, are waiting.

"It's Marky," wheezes Hector. "He's the one. I even have a tape of him on my phone – saying he's going to kill me. Help me, Mammy – I'm going to die."

"No you're not, Hec," says Sandy very gently. "We'll pump you out, and you'll soon be right as rain."

She scowls round at Patsy and Marky. "I'll deal with you later. I can't believe this. You'll both pay for hurting my baby – and pay through the nose."

Patsy shakes her head sadly then covers her eyes in shame. She knows now that Marky is right all along. Eternal vigilance is the price you pay for having money.

*

"So," sighs Harry as they climb the steps onto the new foot-bridge, "how much does she take them for? Nothing less than half-a-mill, by my reckoning."

"Actually," replies Dom, "not a red cent. But only because there is more to come."

"More?"

"Yes. You see, shortly after Hector is admitted to the hospital, Doctor Lovebucket is summoned to deal with another emergency around the corner. So Doc Clancy takes over."

"My pal Doc Clancy?" asks Harry. The old rebel?"

"No his younger brother, Little Doc. He works as a locum in Casualty when they're stuck, ever since Mrs Little Doc ups and leaves him a few years back. Anyhow, Little Doc starts Hector's emetic – and then sends Sandy off to get herself a cup of tea and a bunch of cigarettes to calm herself down, as she's doing his head in. Sandy departs, somewhat reluctantly, blowing air-kisses back at her baby all the while. Unfortunately, Sandy is barely out of the room, when Hector takes a violent seizure and dies."

"Christ," gasps Harry. "And there's me thinking the whole thing is a stick-up job by the mother and son to part poor Patsy from her brass."

"Sandy returns to Casualty, where Little Doc gets her to take a seat and very gently tells her the news. She is astounded, disbe-lieving, and begs Little Doc to let her see her baby. But again, very gently, he tells her that he cannot let her do that – as the area is now a crime scene and that the only person who can see the body now is the police pathologist."

"Sandy screams and screams that she wants her baby, and makes to throttle Little Doc scratching his face with her big long nails. But with that, Doctor Lovebucket, who is weary of the whole show, jabs a little needle into Sandy's fine behind and knocks out her lights."

Harry stops at the middle of the new bridge to admire the magnificent views north towards Donegal and then south towards Tyrone. It also gives him a minute to work on his new hypothesis. He stands, smoking one-half of his daily allowance and gazing into the distance, before finally his face breaks into a grin. "It's payback. Isn't it?"

Dom tips an imaginary hat and nods well done. "As soon as Sandy wakes up, she demands to see the police doctor for permission to see the corpse. So he comes in, along with a uniformed officer – me as it happens. 'How is this possible?' she asks Little Doc, choking back the tears. He tells her that sadly these things happen all the time – particularly when youngsters swallow a big heap of drugs. 'But they're not drugs at all,' she sniffs. 'It's only worm tablets for our little dog – four of them. They'll hardly kill a child, will they? And besides, he never drinks the chocolate – at least not normally he doesn't...'"

"Aha!" laughs Harry.

"My words precisely," says Dom. "So I then ask her where are the real Diazepam. 'Halfway down Patsy Barkley's u-bend,' says she. 'At least, that's where they ought to be...God forgive me, I'm after killing my own son. I'll burn in Hell.' And she then starts to bawl and cry so hard that Little Doc steps in and zaps her out again."

Harry grins. "A little bit mean of you to go that far. I take it the son is totally fine?"

"Right as rain. All this time, they're holding him in a secure cell they use for visiting psychos. Unfortunately, though, he's a year too young for me to arrest – but the mother is a great collar to get. They're going to cut short my training and start me as a probationary detective right away. Hector coughs to the whole lot, when we threaten to take away his phone, and admits that it's their fourth time running this dodge – he reckons Sandy now has more money than a German bank. Doctor Lovebucket – like the other doctors – is just the dupe who makes Hector vomit, when Mammy screams her darling baby is dying."

"How...?"

"It's all thanks to Marky," explains Dom. "He sees Hector palming the Diazepam from the top shelf on the kitchen a few days previously but doesn't challenge him. He's half-hoping the little snake will put them to his head. But then he gets a fit of conscience and rings Curly – who helps me set the whole production up."

"So I take it by that then that you and Curly are back on the best of terms?"

"Never better. In fact she is after sending me a little cake to thank me for all my efforts."

"Very nice of her. It sounds like she's a little sweet on you..."

"Yeah. More than you can imagine. For a joke, I say to her that I'm going to send the cake to Doc Clancy's lab for examination – after he's through with Hector's chocolate drink. But she starts to panic – and says no, no, no, for God's sake, don't do that... So naturally I do. And you'll never guess what's in it?"

"Go on."

"Enough Viagra to kickstart a blown-down telegraph pole. Indeed, Little Doc says that any man who takes even the smallest bite out of that cake will spend the next month taking five steps back from the toilet bowl..."

"Maybe she's dropping you a hint?"

"Possibly – always hard to be sure with Curly."

"Are you going to send it back?"

"God no – never. And let her know I'm onto her? No way. And besides, after the first half-dozen slices, it starts to taste all right..."

The Other Way to Skin a Cat

For Sean M, Genius

Curly Gilmore, the newly-appointed assemblywoman for South Derry, greatly resents the fact her uncle, Harry Hurley MP, only pays her a standard industrial wage. Indeed, she resents it so much that she spends her spare time stealing a similar amount again from him in expenses.

Like all of Harry's troops up at Stormont, the Belfast parliament, Curly must pay her full salary into central party coffers. She then gets a cheque for about half of her bottom-line, leaving her take-home exactly the same as her driver's. But as the dry-skinned accountant always tells her, we're not in it for the money, Comrade.

Happily, Curly has a healthy stash of her own. Her police sergeant father ups and dies a couple of years back, and leaves her a big, big pile – including his cut from several unresolved bank robberies. But there is a matter of principle here too. Curly is talented, works hard, is very highly qualified, and looks like a million dollars. So she is clearly entitled to more.

Harry, however, is worried about the effects of her self-appointed pay hike on morale and tells her as much when they meet for their Saturday breakfast fry at Café Rath Mór in Creggan.

"You don't think they're going to let me know what you're doing?" he asks her, pouring them both tea from the steel pot. "You're claiming full travel mileage to Belfast five days a week – and yet you're living up there, free, in my hotel, and then travelling down home to Derry at the weekend. In my car. Plus, you're trying to extort two hundred quid a week rent for an office that I already own??"

"What do you care? It's not your money."

"I'm afraid it is, Princess. Our days of screwing the state are over. We are the state now. So I have to care."

"I have two law degrees, Harry, and I work seven days a week for you. As a barrister in private practice, I'm worth at least ten times what you're paying me – rising to fifty times if I become a Senior Counsel. And yet at the minute, my net worth to you is exactly the same as the grunt over there guarding the door."

Harry chews his bacon butty slowly then smiles. "Bad example, Curly. That grunt over there has two bullets in his shoulder and a brother in the cemetery. All for me..."

"I'm sorry. You're right, it's a bad example. But there are only so many times you can play the guilt card, Harry."

"And don't I know it. Look, there are ways of dealing with these things. Your problem, Curly is that you lack subtlety. You're too obvious. Look at Dominic, for example. He's living well on a junior policeman's salary, isn't he? Good car, nice house. Ever think about that?"

Curly sniffs; annoyed that Dominic may be holding out on her. "He's not living well enough to take a girl out for a drink..."

"Again with the subtlety, pet. Maybe you need to back off a little and let him come running to you for a change."

"Why, what's he saying? Christ, I hope he's not showing around those photographs..."

She waits for a second before giving Harry a cheeky wink to let him know she's joking. Cameras and camera-phones, like any recording and tracking devices, are a complete no-no in the Hurley family.

She then spears a sausage, smears it in red sauce and decides to bite. "Okay so, how does Dom do it?"

"Easy. He signs over his salary to my broker, who plays the markets for him, at a very significant return."

"How significant?"

"Most weeks, it's exactly a hundred per cent – rising by twenty percent a year, I expect. I'll be very happy to set up the same arrangement for you. But it's us family members only, I'm afraid..."

"You can't just give us the stock tips and let us play for ourselves?"

"Given Dom's record with poker and horses, I'm not sure that's a good idea."

Curly nods her agreement. Dom is a daily communicant at Gamblers Anon and, but for Harry, will still be chasing the rush. She pauses. "I'm not sure that'll work for me, though."

Harry understands. "You're exactly like your mother," he sighs. "You have to do everything for yourself. You won't let anyone help you."

"It's not that at all, Harry," she grins at him. "And I damn sure want the hundred percent rise. It's more that I don't trust you."

*

After the fry, Harry goes to the counter for another pot of tea. And for all his money, he's delighted to get the refill for nothing. He sits back down opposite Curly and braces himself for round two.

"One of my former classmates is now earning five hundred thousand a year in fees, Harry. She's a sharp lass but not half as sharp as me."

"Half a million? At twenty-five? That's hardly possible – unless maybe she's taking the hormones and playing a little football on the side?"

"Nope – all from the law. And may I advise you to keep your comments about transgender sportswomen to yourself. Though, in saying that, someone really needs to talk to her about her shoes... Anyhow, she's just after getting two hundred and fifty grand for one case alone. Just four hours work."

"You're kidding?"

"On my word of honour as a thief, liar and practising lawyer. A quarter of a mill."

"I want to hear this story."

"Okay, but after I make the case for the bar, we're going straight back to the issue of my fees."

"Yeah, like I was getting out of here without you sticking your hand in my pocket..."

*

Winnie McFoster is unusual for a Protestant barrister in that she has no compunction about screwing the establishment. Traditionally, Ulster planter lawyers tend to side rigidly with authority and hold back from putting the boot into their state masters. Catholic lawyers, who have a lifelong suspicion of the same state masters, have no such qualms – and are thus hugely popular among the starving masses.

But Winnie, as Curly rightly suggests, is a sharp young lady. Sharp enough certainly to realise that while it is one thing to be decent and honourable, it is another matter entirely to pay the rent. And the 16th century *castello* that Winnie has her eyes on in Umbria requires quite a hefty rent-cheque indeed. So when one day an old farmer pal of her father's visits and offers her twenty grand to stick one on the taxman, her only question is, How hard do you want me to hit him?

Except it's not quite that simple. Hence the major fee. The problem is that the taxman has caught the farmer cold. Dead cold as it turns out, because the farmer, a lovely gent called Nathan Hall, has only six weeks left to live - and the taxman is about to grab a third of his £7.5 million estate in inheritance taxes. And there is nothing anyone can do about it.

"I have no objection to paying taxes," Nathan tells Winnie. "I'm paying them all my life – on my cattle, pigs, sheep, the milk I sell and whatever wheat is left after I feed the livestock.

"Likewise, I pay taxes on any land I buy or sell. And I pay full taxes for my two sons too, both good honest boys, who work the land with me. But don't get me wrong, I think I get value for my taxes – the schools near me are decent, as are the roads. And the doctors are taking really great care of me, now they finally know what's wrong. Even if they can't get me the medicine I need…"

"What? Why not?"

"Ach, I'm over seventy and the drugs are too dear. And they're sure I'm never going to make it anyway. It's just one of those damn things about getting old, pet. You discover that your life has less value."

"But that's outrageous – you're paying taxes for fifty years."

"I am. And, as I'm telling you, I don't mind that. But, despite paying all these taxes, I always try to save a little as I go. And I'm not too badly off. Asset rich, you know yourself. My plan is always to split whatever I have between the two boys. They're great young men, and I don't care a whit if they sell or stay, because whatever choice they make it'll be right for them. Their mother, God rest her, is dead five years – and between looking after her then, and looking after me now, they deserve nothing but the best.

"All of which is why I am now so angry that the damn government is trying to steal – and as a Presbyterian, steal is a word I rarely use – but they are trying to steal a third of my fortune. All this money is already taxed many times. They have no right whatsoever to tax it again, just because I'm dying."

Actually they do, murmurs Winnie, but not loud enough for Old Nate to hear. Instead she adopts the time-honoured legal trick of whistling through her lips to signify that this is indeed a toughie. "Tell the two boys to come in and see me on Friday morning. It's possible we can write off some of the tax against allowances they may be entitled to."

Nate shakes his head. "That's penny-halfpenny stuff, Winnie. They're about to lose two point five million. And besides, as I keep telling you, all this money is already taxed. I don't want to be paying another dime."

Winnie looks doubtful.

"Tell you what," says the old man. "How about an incentive? Instead of me paying you a flat fee, why don't I give you ten percent of everything you save me? That'll get you thinking."

Winnie sits up and blinks in disbelief. "So if I get you off the hook entirely, you'll give me a quarter mill?"

"Not a cent less. You have my word on that."

And Nate's word, as everyone knows, is good enough to take to the bank. So all of a sudden Winnie's day is becoming very interesting indeed. "You have yourself a deal then. But tell the boys I want to see them on Friday. You come with them. First thing."

"They'll be here."

*

Nate's boys, however, are not quite as pretty as he paints them. And three days later, they don't show up for their date with Winnie. Nate, despite his failing liver, is bang on time - and is shamefaced. "I'm very sorry, Winnie. But they're on a bit of a bender the last couple of days. It's not like them..."

All of a sudden, Winnie starts to feel very sorry for the lonely old man in front of her. He is being let down by those he needs most, just when he needs them most. And she doesn't believe for a minute that this is a new problem. "How long is this going on?" she asks him.

He pauses, realises he's never going to bluff her and decides to give up the story. "Well, they're normally very careful to keep it private. But they drink a bit at home. About a bottle a day each, by my reckoning. But since they know I'm on my way out, they're more blatant about it – they're even starting to use the local pub now."

"A bottle a day? What age are they?"

"Nineteen and eighteen."

"Are they looking after you?"

Nate sighs sadly. "Not really. I'm sure they want to – but they can't cope. They're only children, God love them. And they're both lost souls at the minute – with no mother to guide them through it. Lucky for me, I can afford a nurse."

"So what precisely are they doing as their father lies dying? Are they working on the farm at all?"

"Well, not exactly. Not these last few weeks. The elder fella, Charlie, has a bad back, and the younger boy Sam has this inner ear thing that levels him about once a year."

"So they're on the sick?"

"Yes, but lucky for me, I can afford to hire in some extra hands."

"Do they come back at night to check in on you?"

"Ach, they're just boys. They don't always remember – and sure, I have my nurse anyway."

"Do you think they'll call in sometime today or maybe tonight?"

"I hope so. They're pretty much in full-time residence down at The Orangeman's Rest this last couple of days. But they'll come home again when they need a few pounds."

"Which you'll give them?"

"Darling girl, I have five or maybe six weeks left. What else am I going to do? They're all that's left of me..."

*

But it's not just Winnie who is annoyed. The whole village of Drumbridge, where Nate has his farm, is bristling. Within the space of a short week, Charlie and Sam are no longer welcome at The Orangeman and, instead, are spending their days at the Rebel's Return a low-rent dive on the other side of the square. And it is here that Winnie catches the pair a week after their father's first visit to the office. Each lad is loosely draped around a "streepock" - the preferred local term for a four-drink girl-friend.

"Shame on you," she says. "Bad enough your old man is on his last legs – but you're breaking his heart with all this drinking and whoring about. Take yourselves home, for goodness sake and look after him. Please – he's only a short time left, and he really needs you."

Even as she says the words out loud, Winnie catches herself by surprise. It's not like her at all to care for a client. But Nate is such a good and gentle man.

But the two boys just pretend that she isn't there and continue to suck on their sour whiskeys and sweet hussies. And this sends Winnie into a complete range.

"That's it," she cries. "I'm going back to the farm to talk to your father." And she does.

An hour later, almost to the minute, Winnie pulls her Jaguar up outside the pub again and bursts through the doors with a vengeance. But this time, she has Nate on her arm. The bar, by this stage is pretty packed, but it falls silent as Nate bangs his stick on a table

"Charles and Samuel," he announces, voice faltering, "you're a total disgrace. You're nothing but a pair of thieves – waiting for me to die, so you can ransack my legacy. Well it's not going to happen. I'm cutting you both off. Winnie here has the papers ready. All my money is going to go to the dogs' home. Every cent of it."

Well, the boys' ears prick up at that, and they put down their drinks and women. "We're sorry, Pop," pleads Charlie.

"We truly are," adds Sam. "Please don't do that. It's just we're under, ah, considerable psychological pain…"

"Pain?" gasps Nate. "Let me tell you about fecking pain. I have a third of liver and no working kidney. It's too late boys. Your run on Easy Street is over. Now, go home and get your stuff out of my house, before I get the police."

Somewhere at the back of the bar, a lone set of hands begins to clap. Then it is two, and then four and suddenly eight. And within a minute, everyone in the pub – including the barman and the manager – is clapping and cheering for poor Nate and singing "Cheerio" to his two reprobate sons. They are completely and utterly humiliated and skulk out of the door, red-faced and with heads bowed.

*

The problem with humiliation, however, as any half-decent lawyer will tell you, is that oftentimes the victims don't take their shellacking lying down.

And at nine o'clock the following morning, Winnie McFoster is opening her office door, when a secretary from another law firm rings in to announce that she is going to email her on an emergency writ. Charles and Samuel Hall are going to sue their father for slander – for his remarks in the Rebels Return the previous night. And they are adamant that the matter is to be processed immediately, as their former Pop is about to shuffle off this mortal coil any day now.

The typical lawyer tactic in this situation is to kick for touch – what Winnie's old master Tommy Bowtie refers to as the Three Ds: delay, delay and delay again. But Nate won't hear of it. And, there being no more stubborn client than one who is about to be nailed shut into a wooden box, Winnie is forced to organise a sit-down with Charlie and Sam and their shyster that that same afternoon.

"You're not getting a cent," she begins. "Not one red cent, I tell you."

"We want seven and a half million," replies the boys' shyster, grim-faced.

"That's the value of Nate's entire estate."

"Precisely."

Winnie pauses to negotiate mouth-to-ear with Nate. They scratch chins, whisper intently and then finally nod sombrely together.

"Okay then," Winnie says at last. "You can have it all. We admit liability. It is a terrible slander – and we apologise. The extent of the settlement must remain a private matter – but we think it is fair. Give us a few minutes to get the papers ready."

All parties then shake hands – and within half an hour, Nate is signing away his entire fortune over to his two sons. Tax free.

The only deductions are the 250 grand Nate has to pay Winnie for dreaming up the whole ruse and the twenty grand to the boys' shyster for stringing along.

Nate and his two young boys who love him dearly and protect him forever and for always, go off home happily in the one little car. And none of the three, incidentally, ever appears in a public house or drinks a drop of whiskey from that day to this.

*

Harry tips an imaginary cap to Curly, both in acknowledgement of a good yarn and the fact that smart lawyers are indeed worth their weight in hundred-dollar bills.

He also knows what's coming next and decides to cut her off at the pass.

"I'll do a deal with you," he says, pouring her the last cup from the steel teapot. "Stop trying to rip me off, and I'll cut you in. Properly."

"Why do that?"

"I waste far too much energy keeping an eye you. You're better off inside the gazebo."

Curly smiles modestly, knowing full well she can only win exactly as far as Harry wants her to. "What's the plan, so?"

"Once every so often, I get a wire that someone needs a particular plot of land in a particular area to start up a new business – maybe an American or European investor."

"So?"

"So, if I, or one of my colleagues, can purchase that particular land a short time in advance, it is very likely we will sell it on at a large profit, as soon as the official notices are put in the paper."

Curly furrows her brow, like she's still not sure. "But I'll still have to wait for you to tell me when and where to buy?"

"Unless I appoint you chair of the Stormont Rural Zoning Commission – in which case you may find out even before me..."

"Aha," laughs Curly. "That sounds like quite a promotion for a new girl."

Harry laughs. "It is. But be warned Curly, they'll be watching you like a hawk. Not that you'll need the money for the next while anyway..."

"Why do you say that?"

"Because, princess, last week this old fella, who doesn't want to leave his name, calls me on the phone to thank me so much for all that my niece is after doing for him. And that she deserves every penny of the quarter mill he's after paying her – and even more besides. Oh, and he also insists that there isn't a person alive who knows as much about land law as Curly Gilmore – so to be sure and get her into the right committees up in Stormont to keep an eye on the rest of those crooks."

"I don't know what you're talking about."

"That's what I love about you: you always stick to your story, Winnie."

The Naked Mile

I t is a typical St Patrick's Day morning in Derry. The rain is coming down in sheets, there's a wind whipping in from the Atlantic that could peel the skin off an apple, and the weatherman is offering even money it'll snow before lunchtime. And Dominic Dunne, the rookie detective, could not be happier. "There's no truer test of a man's integrity than his willingness to make good on his marker," he laughs, quoting his uncle Harry's biography word for word.

Harry Hurley, the MP for North Derry, is a lot less chuffed, however. And with good reason. First, as everyone knows, Harry never authorises that damn book in the first place. Second, he's standing in the middle of a media scrum on top of Magazine Gate, one of the walled city's seven historic portals, about to run a one-mile lap of the 17th century ramparts.

And third, and most important of all, he is about to perform this same task...naked. Bollock naked.

"Just remember you're doing it for culture," says Dom, sticking in the knife.

Harry attempts to shoot his nephew a murderous look, sucking in his gut for added tough-guy effect. But he quickly spots that his belly isn't the only thing shrinking in the draught and rapidly lets it sag out again.

To add to his ignominy, the BBC reporter is now standing directly in front of him and beginning his live speech to camera. "Thanks, Sarah. We're here in Derry this morning for one of the more unusual City of Culture preview events, where the MPs Harry Hurley and Victor McCormick, once die-hard enemies, are about to recreate the famous Naked Mile race.

"This contest – originally the brainchild of Frederick Hervey, the 18th Century bishop of Derry – will, depending on the athletes, last between five and fifteen minutes. And while it's no longer an acceptable method of recruiting Church of Ireland curates, to Bishop Hervey's eternal disappointment, ha, ha, today's show-piece will raise about fifty thousand pounds for charity."

The reporter pauses and presses his earpiece to show he's listening. "Ha, ha. You're right, Sarah. There's not a terrible lot to *showpiece* this side of the camera either. But can I just take this opportunity to inform our more sensitive viewers that we do intend to cover the competitors' modesty with little digital shamrocks. Or should I say *tiny* digital shamrocks... In line with tradition, our curates are allowed to fortify themselves with a drink at the starting line. Though I'm just hearing in my ear, that the Teetotallers' Association will donate another thousand pounds to charity, if neither gentleman fuels up on alcohol."

"Stuff them," snaps Harry, right into the camera. "They're not the ones standing with their vegetables in the ice-box. I'll chip in that grand myself. Now where's my naggin of Brandy?"

"They can have a grand from me too," says Vic McCormick, a huge bear of a man, who like Harry is also suffering from a severe proportionality complex. "Bring me my Bushmills."

The two men clink bottles and drink avidly.

"You ready?" Vic asks him at last.

Harry has a last minute idea and turns quickly to his nephew Dominic. "Will you run alongside me with the umbrella?"

"Love to, Harry – but I'm afraid I'm not allowed."

The BBC man smirks in agreement: "Yeah. We're chipping in a grand of our own to get full unblemished footage. Or rather 'inch-age' in your case."

Harry realises he has nothing at hand with which to strike the reporter, so instead he grits his teeth and heads for the starting line. A crack like that in the old days, and the BBC man will be wearing his microphone as a popsicle-stick. "Okay then," he groans. "Let's get this thing over with. Last one home, Vic, gets to sleep with your wife..."

*

The pistol goes bang and the runners break into a slow trot up the walls towards Castle Gate. A posse of about twenty frightening-looking stewards, consisting of some of Vic and Harry's top soldiers in wet-weather running gear, automatically impose a ten-foot perimeter around the MPs.

"Anybody from the press who encroaches on the circle will be asked to leave the walls," says Gerry Hurley, Harry's brother, pointing downwards at the twenty-foot drop to Magazine Street. No-one doubts him for a second – though they're all secretly hoping that the BBC man will give it a try.

The cortege shuffles slowly up the hill past the Tower Museum, one of the top facilities in Europe according to a recent vote - and now housing a world-famous exhibition of the proud Spanish Armada's valiant defeat at the hands of the merciless Elizabethans.

Vic, a lifelong smoker, is already in trouble and taps Harry on his bare shoulder to slow down.

"This is all your fault," he wheezes.

"No way, Vic. You can't hang all this on me. Neither of us have clean hands here. I'm telling you from day one that this City of Culture contest is not going to end well for us."

"True – but I'm not the big idiot who promises that, if the city wins this award, he'll personally lead one of the key events."

"No, but you are the big idiot who agrees with him..."

"That's because I'm one hundred percent sure it will never happen. My people will never buy into anything which removes the 'London' from Londonderry."

"Persackly. Just as my people will never take buy into any contest for best 'British' city. And besides, the organisers will never allow us to win this thing anyway – we're far too dangerous."

The two men laugh bitterly.

"Shows how much we know," says Vic. "You don't think this is their plan all along?"

"Of course it is," says Harry. "It's the one abiding rule of politics and warfare: anything you can dream up, no matter how crazy or off the wall, the opposition is already doing."

*

Truth is, Harry is nervous since the very first minute he hears of the contest, three years ago. He can sniff a set-up better than a fat dog smells sausages. And he knows he has to kill off the whole contest malarkey before it even gets out of the traps.

The prize, for the uninitiated, is to become the first UK City of Culture. And Harry's followers will always resist any bid to label Derry a 'UK' city. After all, his hometown is the crown of Ireland. But Harry is equally aware that there is considerable prestige, and money, to be made if the contest goes their way. Derry's profile will shoot up, and everything from tourism to industry will enjoy a payday the likes of which the city may never see again. So, as with all such matters, there is serious potential for a split in the camp.

For all that, Harry's common-sense tells him it's never going to happen: Derry is too small, too risky and too unloved to win such a competition. And besides, there are thirty-odd real British cities in the contest with very strong claims to the title.

Try as he may, though, he is just not able to wish it away.

Accordingly, the day that Derry makes the City of Culture shortlist of four, Harry rings Vic for a sitdown in the comfortably neutral surrounds of the Everglades Hotel.

"Do we want this to win?" he asks Vic, directly.

"Officially yes," answers Vic. "There is only one political answer that doesn't involve us being crucified, as these tricky sods know well."

"And unofficially?"

"Absolutely not. It'll just be the same old story. You and I will end up killing one another for a few crumbs, while the carpetbaggers from Belfast, Dublin and London will clean out the coffers. The Brits will then blame us for the entire mess, 'We do our best – we give and we give and we give, but there's just no working with these people.' And then me and you will go and do something stupid that no-one will ever forgive us for."

Harry smirks. "I'm with you one hundred percent. But listen, Vic, I may have an idea. Their rules say any entry must have council backing."

"They'll get that no problem."

"What if we stir things a little?"

Vic bites his lip. "They'll never let us away with it."

"It doesn't have to come from us..."

Vic smiles darkly. Like Harry, peacetime bores the pants off him, so he's always up for a spot of rakery. "Okay then. Let's give it a go. Here's what we'll do - why don't I get my boys to float some festival events for that are so true blue and British that your men will be digging up their kitchen floors looking for their guns again?"

"And I'll get my lot to float a few ideas so green and Irish that your boys will be marching all the way back to the Boyne."

"They'll end up tearing each others' throats out."

"Per-sackly. And they'll turf the whole shebang in the bin."

Vic laughs. "You're a genius, Big H. They'll have to get up early to catch us boys out..."

*

The first quarter of their run passes without incident, other than the predictable catcalls from the Georgian shops and offices on Magazine Street. But when Gerry the Hurler pulls out his iPhone and begins photographing the biggest noise-makers, the volume goes down considerably.

At Butcher Gate, the posse pause for a quick breath opposite the glass-fronted Calgach Conference Centre, until the 400 children, who are in there for a cross-community choir competition, spot them and start hammering on the windows.

"Your Catholic youngsters are a lot rowdier than my Protestants," sniffs Vic.

"That's because they've a lot more to cheer on," explains Harry, lowering his head proudly.

They trundle on slowly past the First Presbyterian Church, a just-restored neo-classical landmark. Then it's up towards the Apprentice Boys Memorial Hall, an imposing Gothic edifice, that now houses the finest museum of loyalist paraphernalia on the island.

A few dozen men in orange sashes are waiting outside the hall, to issue ribald remarks at Harry and Vic as they skulk past. But this time the race stewards take no pictures, as these guys are tough enough to take on Gerry the Hurler's entire protection detail and are very possibly carrying, besides.

The sash-wearers, all former buddies of Vic's, are big supporters of the City of Culture bid from day one. Their museum is bound to become a major focal point for visitors – and they aren't happy at all at their boss is trying to queer the pitch. So Harry and Vic are forced to take their abuse on the chin and other vulnerable parts.

And so, they stumble on towards the source of all their troubles. Fifty yards further up the ramparts is a giant empty plinth overlooking the Bogside. And as they pass it, Harry and Vic look at one another and shake their heads forlornly.

"Next time, we'll leave well enough alone," says Vic.

"Yes," agrees Harry, "but let's face it, next time, there will be no next time."

*

It is Vic's bright idea to restore the statue of Governor Walker to the empty plinth. He reckons that the return of the 300-year-dead Protestant icon onto his platform, as one of the central City of Culture events, will irk the residents of the Bogside who live below a great deal. And then some. So much so, they will say to hell with your Culture plan, Harry, and demand nothing to do with it.

Of course, Vic is far too cute to have his fingerprints on this idea, and instead asks his woman on council, Sue Clarke, to propose it. So she does – albeit very reluctantly, as there is no money calling the Pope a cross-dresser when you live in Vatican City. But, while Vic's planters vote en bloc to restore the world's greatest ever Fenian-beater to his pedestal, as expected, Harry's troops respond with a resounding 'nay'. And this being Derry, the proposal is roundly defeated.

Harry's people aren't happy at all at this attempted, disrespectful one-upmanship, however, and launch a counter-proposal of their own, which they claim is in the best keepings of the city's cultural heritage. They will, on second thoughts, agree to the statue being replaced on its plinth, on condition that they can re-enact a forty-year-old event from their own culture. To wit, they will place a bomb under the structure – and blow it all the way into the Bogside. Just like back in '73.

This motion is passed by a simple council majority, but only as a lesson to Vic, who everybody knows is pulling the strings. No-one really wants things that go bang in the night any more.

But the proposal and counter-proposal cause no little friction between the various strands in Derry, who are previously doing all right together this long time when Vic and Harry leave them alone. The row also causes considerable public embarrassment for the city as the media are suggesting that Derry's main cultural talent is in dragging the rest of the world back into the Dark Ages.

Indeed, the last council meeting ends in a serious bit of handbags, after Sue Clarke attempts to fell Harry's brother, Gerry the Hurler, with her council-issue laptop. Unfortunately, she ends up whiplashing her own deputy, Jilly Gillespie instead, when she forgets to unplug it first. But Jilly, thankfully, is all right, apart from a bump on her forehead which the council will pay her five grand to keep quiet about.

After the debacle, which thankfully takes place in Confidential Business and not in front of the press, Gerry calls Sue in for a private meeting to thrash things out and apologise for his earlier cracks about her weight. And the upshot of this is that both council leaders return to their respective bosses, Harry and Vic, and demand that they keep their damn noses out of local business.

To twist the rope a little tighter, Gerry also arranges a BBC radio interview for Harry the next day – ostensibly a safe bitching session about health cuts – and gets the interviewer to lob in a little grenade about the Culture competition. Do you want us to win this thing, Harry, yes or no? Let's get it on the record.

And Harry, who is convinced that Derry's chances are now damaged beyond repair by the statue shenanigans, says yes, yes, yes, as enthusiastically as the blonde librarian on his favourite late night channel.

"Indeed," continues Harry tongue planted in cheek, "if there is any way I can demonstrate my commitment to the campaign, I will do it."

"How about taking part in one of the keynote events – as a player?" counters the radio man, quickly.

"Absolutely. Just name the day, and I'll be there. I really hope we win."

Harry sighs inwardly, realising that he is just after offering a penalty kick to Fate.

The interviewer, however, then decides to get himself a two-fer, and puts it to Harry that much of the recent trouble is down to the loyalist side – i.e. it's Vic's fault and his people won't be taking part in any celebrations anyway. But Harry realises that this gives Vic a get-out clause, and there is no way that Harry is going to be left swinging in the wind alone.

"No, no," says Harry. "The loyalist leader Victor McLaughlin is in total agreement with me on this matter – he says so all the time. And I'm sure that he will take part in any and all keynote events as well."

As he hangs up his mobile after the interview, Harry stops briefly to open the incoming text from Vic. It contains just one word: "Lundy."

Lundy, as Harry is well aware, is a former governor of Derry, who is burned every year in effigy from the old plinth on the walls by Vic's people, for attempting to sell out the city during the siege of 1689. And in Vic's circles, the insult is about as rough as they come.

*

The runners take their second break at the top of the hill by the Double Bastion – home of Roaring Meg, the biggest of the city's unequalled collection of 17th century cannons. From the high ramparts here, on a clear day, it is possible to view the rolling, six-mile sprawl of the new city outside the walls, from Mullenan to Culmore.

With the right tour guide, you can pick out the homes of great writers like Deane, McCafferty and McCann; or you can survey the old College, which includes Nobel laureates like Hume and Heaney and Tony-winners like Friel among its old boys. If you are of a political bent you can check out the streets of Free Derry and Creggan, battleground for much of the early Troubles; or if you simply like a bit of scenery, you can admire the host of new landmarks from the Gasyard Centre to Celtic Park GAA ground, to Creggan Country Park and the university.

None of this, however, remotely interests either Vic or Harry, who are cold, wet, tired and in serious need of their hip flasks. Given that neither gent has a hip pocket, however, they are forced to call on their seconds to provide them with a snifter.

They both sit down on the damp steps leading up to the bastion and drink deeply. Harry glowers at his brother Gerry and shakes his head in disgust. Sue Clarke, Vic's number two, grins as her boss attempts to replicate Harry's glare but fails.

The day after Harry's radio interview, the council votes unanimously to support the City of Culture idea – with Sue and Gerry generously giving full credit for the turnaround to their respective party leaders, Vic and Harry.

"Traitors," mutters Vic, still eyeing their deputies.

"Not as bad as Curly, though," says Harry.

"No," agrees Vic. "Your niece is a class apart."

Harry's fallback position, after the radio debacle, is to lean on his sister's daughter, Curly Gilmore to foul things up for the Culture competition at Stormont, the next layer of government up the ladder.

Curly is the new assemblywoman for North Derry - and Harry's eyes and ears at the Belfast parliament. So, he instructs her to table a motion there outlawing the use of the term "London-derry" in any and all official and unofficial correspondence per-taining to the city. And this will come into effect, if it passes, on January 1, 2013, the first day of the City of Culture year.

This, naturally, is like waving a red flag in the face of the con-test's UK organisers before asking them to touch their toes so we can insert the flagpole rectally. And there is no way they will award Derry the crown, if they are going to behave like this.

But Curly refuses to be a patsy for the cause and turns down Harry's proposal. Flat. Indeed she even offers to resign from the party and advise everyone what Harry is attempting to do, if he persists.

Harry wonders if this is because his nephew Dominic – a former Oxford scholar who is very pally with Curly – is such a fan of cul-ture. Curly, he is certain, is more than a little smitten with Dom and will do anything he asks her. But when he puts this to her, she simply informs him, as she often does, that he is too bent on proving himself right and never bent enough on doing the right thing.

"You're just like all the little emperors," she tells him, "if you can't be in charge of the toys, then no-one else can play. And for someone else to come into your sandbox and start lining up the horsies – it just breaks your dark little heart."

Harry rejects this roundly, and launches in to a diatribe about the cunning Brits attempting to civilise the natives by stealth. But Curly is already out the door, and he is left talking to an empty chair.

*

Between you, me and the wall, though, both Dom and Curly are playing more of a behind-the-scenes role in the culture campaign than anyone could guess.

Very much on the qt, Dom is back to his old tricks and is after gambling a full year of his salary on Derry getting the culture award – at a cool fifteen-to-one. Large odds, indeed, seeing as there are only four on the shortlist.

But Barry the Bookie is only too happy to indulge Dom, knowing well that this client is as unlucky a gambler as ever borrows breath. And besides, Oxford – the city of dreaming spires, Isaac Newton and Morse - is number one on the shortlist and a racing favourite.

Dom, it appears, is the victim of inside information, which is after going out of date. About three months ago, he is in contact with an old university buddy, who is helping run Oxford's campaign. And this guy assures Dom they are really worried that Derry will beat them. But this, of course, is before all the nonsense about the statue and the subsequent write-ups in the paper.

So when Dom returns to Barry's offices wanting to know if he can cancel all, or even a little small part of his wager, he gets the predictable one-fingered response.

"Listen, Barry," he pleads, "these are extraordinary circumstances. Isn't there something in the rule book about acts of God?"

"Sorry partner," says Barry, "acts of God are one thing, acts of stupidity are another."

"But the city is totally out of the running. Even the prime minister is saying so. There's more of a chance of Harry running bare-assed around the city walls, than there is of us winning the title."

"Tell you what, so," laughs Barry, "I'll give you a hundred-to-one against that ever happening."

Dom stares at him for a minute, thinks it over, then nods slowly. "You're on, so. I'll risk another grand. You'll take my cheque?"

"Absolutely, Dom," grins Barry. "Immediately after you take it down to the bank and convert it to cash."

"All right then," says Dom, "I'll do that". And the two men shake hands. But Barry has a bad, bad feeling.

*

The runners scale the steps at the top of Bishop's Gate, skirt quickly past the Fountain and begin the slow descent down the ramparts towards the river.

The whiskey and brandy are starting to do their job. The rain seems to be biting a little less, and both Harry and Vic are starting to believe that they might actually survive the experience.

As they pass St Columb's Cathedral, a magnificent gothic edifice – and the first Protestant cathedral built anywhere on the islands after the Reformation, they slow down to walking pace out of respect. And as they do, Curly Gilmore emerges from a large throng who are looking on from the church graveyard and laughing loudly.

The pretty young assemblywoman, hops up the steps onto the walls, gives her uncle a big thumbs-up by way of hello, then bounds past him to kiss Dominic on the cheek.

"Don't forget our big date tonight," she tells him.

"I won't," laughs her second cousin. "A deal is a deal."

Harry glances sideways at the pair, focusing his bloodshot eyes on his nephew first. "What deal? You're going to go out with her? What about your 'no incest' rule?"

"I checked with Father Adlous – we're far enough apart on the tree. And besides, it's only one dinner."

Unable to shake an answer out of Dom, he turns sharply to his niece. "What's this deal he's talking about then? If it's anything to do with me, I'll have your skin."

Curly is used to her uncle and barely blinks. "Calm yourself, Harry. It has nothing to do with you. And besides, you've more than enough skin of your own to be getting along with. Apart from that little bare patch down there, which no-one knows about until today..."

Harry bites his lip and counts to ten. There's little to be gained in throttling an MLA in front of a live TV camera. Instead, he turns to Vic beside him and shakes his head disconsolately. "You ever feel you're just pawns in someone else's game, buddy?"

"Never more so than today," nods Vic.

Curly chuckles and points back to the old cathedral. "You know that big spire there is Bishop Hervey's idea? When the cathedral first goes up in the 1630s, the church roof is as flat as an old joke – but Hervey has a fine eye for these things and argues that it'll be nicer with a spire. So in the late 1700s, he gets permission and sticks on the new bit."

Harry glares at her, as various pieces start falling into place in his head. "How come you're such an authority on Bishop Hervey?"

"Whoops," laughs Curly, taking Dom's arm. "I better say no more or I'll give the game away…"

*

As they enter the theatre quarter, Dom peels off from the crowd on the walls to visit Barry the Bookie's private office in the nearby Foyleside shopping centre and collect his winnings.

Barry is as sore as only a wrong-footed bookie can be. But he pays up to the nickel, after the detective reminds him he is exactly one endorsement away from losing his licence.

"You know I'm going to get it all back from you – and the same again," he tells Dom, as he hands over the cheque. "I always do."

"Not this time, you won't," vows Dom. "My betting days are over."

"You can't resist it. You need the buzz."

Dom is about to argue some more but decides to leave his old adversary with a moral victory. There is nothing to be gained by telling Barry that he is still working the twelve-step programme every day.

But Barry, who is an expert at spotting a tell, sees it in Dom's face anyway and flares up. "No fair, Dom. I'm not having this. You can't just opt back in for sure things and then opt back out again. That's not how we do business."

"Actually, Barry, it is. And I'm going to. And I'm only taking back from you precisely what's mine anyway – not a cent more."

Barry's eyes narrow. "In which case, I'm going to tell Harry the whole thing is a set-up. The contest, the Naked Mile race, the lot – and that you're running it as one dirty big dodge. Then we'll see how smart you are. Unless you kick back my money, of course..."

Dom smiles gently at the bookie. He's after taking him for four very big notes – three on the Derry winning the contest on the other one on Harry's bare-assed marathon - so he doesn't want to go jamming a pencil in his eye as well.

"You can tell whoever you want, Barry," says Dom. "But for what it's worth, Curly is giving Harry the good news face to face, right as we speak. Both of us are hoping to do it, but she beats me in the toss."

Barry shakes his head in disgust. "Okay then – we'll go a bit broader. Gerry the Hurler and the boys won't like it when they hear you're hitting me for four hundred kilos and they're not getting any of it."

Dom shrugs in agreement. "You're right. Very right. But you don't seriously think this is a one man job? You don't for one minute believe I'm greedy enough to keep all this action for myself? Check with your pals in the online bookshops. One hour before the betting closes on the City of Culture contest, more than a million sobs find their way right onto Derry's nose. I'm no sole trader, Barry. This, my friend, is what is termed a community enterprise."

Barry takes a deep breath as he works it all out. Payback, as he knows from many years of doling it out, is all the more unpleasant when there is no court of appeal.

But it is vital to Barry's business that he will know the score for again. So, he swallows back his anger and his pride, and he affects a rueful smile. "Tell me, Dom, please. How does it work?"

Dom nods okay. "Well the secret of all successful propositions is to know the result before your opponent – in this case you."

"Yes, but no-one knows who's going to win the City of Culture award."

"Precisely. Except, perhaps, for one of my old poker-playing buddies from college, who is compiling Oxford's entry form. And he incidentally, is just after buying himself a new top-of-the-range BMW."

"Aha. So it's like that."

"It is indeed. You see, unfortunately my old pal is a rotten speller and he forgets to spell check the entry form before submitting it. His grammar isn't great either. And the judges take a very dim view of things like that – they reckon it's not terribly cultural at all."

"And I'm never getting my cheque back, then?"

"No. Now, do you want to hear the rest of the story?"

"Of course I do. Please proceed."

*

"The problem," Curly tells Harry, as he jogs slowly down past the redeveloped Playhouse Theatre complex, "is that the judges are livid at you for messing with the contest. They want to give the prize to Derry on merit – they actually believe the city deserves it. They reckon we have more singers per square foot than any other city on the planet – not to mention our poets, novelists, playwrights, film-makers and artists. It's just like the old joke - if you fire a bullet anywhere in Derry, you're going to hit two musicians – the guy you are aiming at, and the bass-player tapping him for loose change.

"But with you and Vic, culture comes down to proving to the world that this is your town - and that you can pee highest up its walls. So, after your attempts to recreate the decimation of Walker's Statue go south, we hear through the mill that the judges are reconsidering their first option – and that our only sure chance of winning now is if we can silence you both once and for all."

Harry pauses briefly, as they pass between St Columb's Hall, an old haunt of Jim Reeves, and the new Millennium Forum. Vic is still three hundred yards back up the hill, throwing up his porridge outside the 18th century Talbot Theatre.

"It's not that we're against this contest," Harry begins, "but..."

"No-one doubts it," interrupts Curly. "And you're right – we have to make sure those thieving opportunists from Belfast don't steal away our clothes. If you can forgive the metaphor. And the judges know this too and will help us. But, as part of the deal of us getting the award, we have to assure your buy-in. Publicly and permanently.

"To that end, myself and Dom have a little chat with Gerry and Sue, who are really tired carrying the can for your nonsense at council. And they generously agree to give their full backing to the campaign, so long as we can devise one major cultural show-piece, which all sides will back."

Harry nods grudgingly. "Hence the Naked Mile... I have to say, it's a new one on me, though."

Curly winks. "Yeah, it's possible it's just a legend. Between you and me, we still can't find any historical record of it. But when Dom mentions that the story is kicking about university while he is over there, both Gerry and Sue offer to forge the appropriate documents – and then stand over them with their lives. Then of course, they bring it to a confidential council committee who endorse it with the first one hundred percent vote in thirty years."

Harry closes his eyes in horror. This just keeps getting better and better. Eventually, he exhales deeply and smiles at his niece. "Question, how much are you going to make from this?"

"Three very big ones, between myself and Dom. Gerry, Sue and their buddies? A lot more, I suspect. But Dom is the only person who has money on you running round the walls in your naked pelt – scores us another big one. Dom even makes Barry the Bookie think it's his idea. God, I love that man."

"And to put a tin hat on it, you're getting you dinner with him - at long last."

"Yeah, for helping him pull this off. And a girl can do a lot of damage in one dinner."

"I don't doubt it – particularly if the girl is you."

*

The finish line at the top of Magazine Gate is now in sight. And Harry slows down as he passes the Guildhall – Derry's landmark tribute to Big Ben and the venue for city council meetings.

"You know the organ upstairs is the biggest in Europe," quips Curly.

Harry is far too long in the game to reply. There is no smart remark on earth that can save him now. Still, he realises that little more harm can come to him, so he stops to wave at the hundreds of St Patrick's Day revellers gathered in the square below - and who can only see his top half.

"It's not so bad, now," he tells Curly. "I've enough brandy in me to fuel a small riot – and at least I'm going to finish the race unlike Vomiting Victor there."

He grins at his niece then waves hello to Dominic, who is back waiting for him at the tape, large bottle in one hand, tinfoil blanket in the other.

"For your own sake," he whispers to her, "don't let him start gambling again. He's far too good a guy to let it wreck him."

"Don't worry Uncle H," she laughs. "I intend to give him a different buzz entirely."

"I'm sure you will...One more question that's bothering me, though. I can clearly remember you and Dom coming to me and Vic and telling us about this run. In fact, I can remember it as if it's just yesterday."

"So?"

"And I recall us both agreeing to it, on the grounds that it is traditional, it is cross-community and that every dog's arse will give money to charity if we do it."

"And, of course, the fact that you owe us for jeopardising the bid..."

"– I accept that. But at no stage - and again, I have to stress again, I have a great memory for detail - does anything come to mind about Vic and I having to run without any clothes. Until the day it first appears in the newspapers, that is."

"By which stage, the entry forms are already in..."

"Per-sactly. In fact, in those early days, I recall you referring to it as the 'Curates' Mile' – no mention of nakedness whatsoever."

"You're quite possibly correct, Uncle Harry. But you know better than anyone always to read the fine print."

"I do now – even in oral agreements."

Curly pats Harry's back as he breaks the tape and raises his arms mock-triumphantly. "Well done," she tells him, "now go and get some clothes on."

"What's all that about?" asks Dom her, as he hands Harry over his various life-savers.

"I'm just telling him about our date," she replies.

"Oh," says Dom. "What about it?"

"Well, you know the way I'm totally in charge for tonight."

"Yes. I have all your texts and emails."

"And you know the way some girls might expect you to dress for dinner?"

"I do."

"Well, I don't…"

"So it'll just be casual, so?"

"Not quite, Dom."

"What then?"

She smiles happily at her new boyfriend and winks a beautiful brown eye that will never stop adoring him. "You'll find it in the small print. I think I'll let Harry explain this one…"

Curly and the Fatman

"If there is a hillier city in Ireland than Derry, it remains damn well hidden," Harry Hurley MP tells his nephew Dominic Dunne as they stand at the bottom of Southway and gaze up.

For today's lunchtime walk, Harry wants to climb the winding mountain-road leading from the Brandywell Stadium to Piggery Ridge at the top of Creggan and, if God spares him, make it all the way back down again. It's only about three miles on paper, but the first kilometre of the route is so sheer that road-racers refer to it as the 'The Killer K'.

"From here, it looks even steeper than my car insurance," laughs Dominic, the rookie cop, who is just one more gotcha away from his very own 12-month speeding ban.

"It's still not as bad as Creggan Hill," says his uncle, starting round the corner. "If you're ever suffering from constipation, just try coming down there some icy day with no snow-tyres. You'll be shooting on all cylinders in no time. Some of the older ones still call Creggan Street 'Thundering Down', an account of the way the rainwater gushes down in torrents. Just like a water-fall."

Dominic shakes his head. "Fountain Hill in the Waterside is steeper again. At least once a week, I'm over there mopping up bits of some teenage cyclist or roller-blader. Or if I'm really lucky, I'll even get to pull a skate-boarder out of a parked car. It's a rites of passage thing – for the boys that make it, that is."

"My old mate Chrissy Lateshift still live over there?"

"Sure does," laughs Dom, "still taxiing away. Always comes out to say hello. Must be seventy now."

"–Try eighty. I'm sure by now you know all about his former next-door neighbour, Sean McDobbin?"

"No. What's the story there?"

Harry stops momentarily to stare back at the two hundred yards stretch he's after climbing, and shakes his head in sorrow at how little it is.

"Ach it's a famous old yarn – can't believe you don't know it. McDobbin is this little hunchback guy – an evil-tempered little so-and-so. The type who bites you if you speak to him and bites you if you don't. Anyway, he ups and dies about forty years back, and, as is the form, they decide to wake him from the front room of his house.

"–Tricky old walk with a coffin on that hill."

"Per-sackly. And funny you saying that, because there's a real problem with getting McDobbin into the coffin in the first place. Due to the curvature of his spine, when they lay him out flat, his top half is at ninety degrees to his legs – it's like he's sitting up waiting to greet you. 'Course this will scare the life out of the locals, half of whom already believe he is a demon. So they send for Old Doc Clancy to see if there's anything he can do."

"Is that Clancy the Rebel or Little Doc?"

"Neither, their old da – Papa Doc. A great character too. Anyhow, Papa Doc comes in to the wake-room, surveys the corpse and suggests that they need to get a big belt and tie McDobbin down into the coffin, which they do. And after the undertaker prettifies things with a few veils and a set of rosary beads, no-one is any the wiser."

Harry stops again as they round the first big u-bend on the hill outside Termonbacca Monastery. He can feel his legs starting to cramp up already but will never admit this to his nephew, so he feigns a shoelace emergency. Dom, however, spots what is going on and tactfully resolves to slow the pace.

"Anyway," continues Harry, both shoes rectified, "the wake finally gets underway at McDobbin's house and a decent crowd assembles outside. But despite Mrs McDobbin's efforts, no-one wants to go in to see the corpse. They're all too afraid of him. They reckon that if Seany was such an evil little git alive, what's he going to be like now he's dead? So eventually, the poor widow has to send for a priest to put them right."

"Who do they get?"

"Father Aldous from Chapel Road. He's the nearest. So, he comes down, drags everybody from the front street into the wake-room and proceeds to read them the riot act. Tells them shame on you for believing in all this superstitious nonsense. Shame on you being scared of this poor, defenceless critter. And shame on you for maligning this poor dead soul.

"But, as the words are coming out of his mouth, outside the front door a lorry is hurtling down Fountain Hill at a fierce rate of knots, rattling every window and floorboard in the house. And doesn't the belt holding down poor McDobbin snap in two under the pressure, causing the corpse to leap up suddenly out of the coffin.

"'Holy Christ,' cries the crowd, as they bolt for the door. But they're all beaten to the handle by Father Aldous whose last words to the room are: 'Keep away from me, you evil hunchback bastard!'"

*

As they reach St Peter's School, the slope begins to level out a little. Harry's face is a little red so Dominic calls for a break, ignoring his uncle's claims that he can go on all day. Harry sits himself on a dry-looking wall and sparks up the first half of his daily cigarette allowance.

"They'll kill you," warns Dom.

"Maybe," laughs Harry. "But they'll be at the end of a very long queue."

Dom perches himself beside Harry and gazes down the mountain at one of the sweetest views in Ireland: the dark River Foyle weaving its way through the woodlands and lush green valleys, out towards Donegal.

Harry, as is his procedure, then looks over both his shoulders before lowering his head to speak out the side of his mouth. "We have a problem with one of our drivers, Dom, and I need you to help. But quietly."

"Go on."

"Our taxi-men make a decent living, not a great one. So sometimes, they do little jobs on the side that aren't exactly part of their contract."

"Like booze-runs?"

"Precisely. But if we catch them at it, we drum them out. No second chances. Back in the old days, they'll get a battering too – or maybe even worse – but we're not allowed to do that anymore. Anyhow, our drivers have to set the example, and if they start acting the maggot, every cabbie in Derry will begin following suit. This case, however, isn't just a matter of ferrying a couple of bottles of vodka to a student party. It's a lot worse."

"Drugs?"

"'Fraid so. But not just the recreational stuff – the heavy goods as well. And on a pretty large scale."

"How many drivers?"

"Just the one that we know of."

"Why not make it official and call the police in properly?"

"Because then it becomes a thing. And if this guy ever comes before a judge, he'll start singing all sorts of songs about the old days. And that, as you'll gather, will do neither myself nor my taxi-business, any good whatsoever."

"You know who it is, so?"

"Oh yes. And he has plenty of insurance."

"You and he go way back?"

"Far too far back."

"Have you a Plan B?"

"Absolutely not. As I say, we're not allowed to do that anymore. And if this guy gets wind of anything stirring in the grass, he'll be leaving post mortem letters with every solicitor in the country."

"Does he know you're onto him?"

"Strongly doubt it. He runs a very tight ship – trusts no-one. He only connects with two other people directly, and they do virtually all the day-to-day business for him. And they're both very clean – and are so scared of him that they'll never give him up."

"So, what you're looking for is something that'll rattle him so hard that he'll crawl off into the grass and never come back?"

"Per-sackly."

"Tough one, but leave it with me."

*

Curly Gilmore, who is both Dominic's oldest friend and newest girlfriend - and incidentally Harry's niece, doesn't like the new mission one bit. And she tells Dom as much, when he calls into her office for a cup of coffee after his shift.

"Harry needs to clean the crap out of his own nest first. The biggest pushers in this town are the publicans, and he's the big daddy of all of them. Ninety percent of my private practice court-work is drink-related – from spousal murder to shoplifting and back. Coke and speed are small potatoes. What I make from drugs cases in a year doesn't buy me a decent pair of shoes."

Dom purses his lips, well aware that she has a point – but knowing equally well this is one job he can't get himself out of. "C'mon Curly, it's not just about the drugs. It's all about a lieutenant promoting himself to captain, without the general's say-so."

"So the general gets my boyfriend to head up a secret firing squad? Because you and I know, Dom, this is how it's going to end. And Harry, once again, will be the saviour of his people."

"–No, there'll be none of that. He's pointing me towards permanent exile. If he needs the other, he'll call in Uncle Gerry and leave me well out of it."

"Maybe he wants to have something on you?"

"–No. He knows there can't be a whiff of anything. Not off their number one man in the new police force."

"So, who's the lucky victim?"

"Fatman O'Fallon. Sometimes known as Father Fatman on account of the fact that he reads so many guys their last rites."

"No way. Fatman is one of the old nutting squad? He's such a civil fella too."

"You know him?"

"Drives me to Belfast once a week. He's on the rota."

Besides her lawyering, Curly is a parliamentarian for Harry up at Stormont – a job she will take a lot more seriously when they pay her what she's worth.

Dom stares directly into her soft brown eyes, almost afraid to ask the next question. "You don't ever...you don't ever buy from him, do you?"

Like many high-achievers in their mid-twenties, Curly has her own particular ways of unwinding at the weekend. These include chasing various buzzes where she can find them – though more recently, it's all Dom.

"Is that a deal-breaker?" she asks, momentarily taken aback by the force of his steely blue glare.

Dom knows it is both way too early and way too late in their friendship for him to answer that question, so he drops the cop act and lowers his gaze.

"Who's with him?" she asks, changing the subject.

"Two Polish guys, so says Harry. They're not ours, so we've no interest in them."

Curly understands. There's no money in starting fights with strangers. "Listen, Dom, don't involve yourself in this one. Leave Fatman to me. I may just be able to handle things with a quiet word."

Curly is one of only two people in the city that Dom, with his Oxford degree, accepts is smarter than him. She is possibly even as smart as Harry. But he also knows she has an agenda of her own here.

"You have a fortnight," he says at last. "That's as long as I can hold Harry off."

"A month," she corrects him abruptly. "And you're good at holding things off. This girl I know, it takes her ten years before she can score one lousy date with you."

"Yeah, but only because I know there will never be any other dates with any other girls ever again, lousy or otherwise."

"So it's like that, is it?"

"You know very well it is, Curly. After you, I'm ruined for all comers..."

His words tail off as he gives her a minute to read the subtext. It's out there now and too late to call back. And for all her decade-long stalking of him, he's still not sure how she'll take it. Be careful what you pray for, and all that. But the glow off her face gives her away.

"You can be very sweet for a tough guy," she smiles, suddenly soft. "And you can take that look of panic off you – the same goes for me too. There never can and never will be anyone else. It's crazy even to try. Now, take me out of these handcuffs so I can give you a proper hug...And besides, it's your turn to be the prisoner. I want to be the detective slapping you with a ruler for a change. So, bend over that table, and confess how much you love me, bitch."

*

A fortnight later, Dom and Harry are in the Old Library Trust in Creggan, enjoying a sandwich after their quadruple-lap of the Bishop's Field football pitches next door. Harry loves the views from up here on the mountain summit, but after his last adventure on the Killer K, he is of the firm belief that it is not always necessary to travel up by foot.

He surveys the busy café, works out no-one is interested in him and begins talking into his tuna melt.

"How's the thing going with Fatman?"

"No change as yet," says Dom. "He keeps it too tight. Why are you asking?"

"No particular reason – let's just say there's a bit of a rush on it. We're thinking of pulling in one of the Poles, see if we can squeeze him. Get him to set Fatman up."

"That's a dangerous road. What if he comes straight to us at the station? You'll have all sorts of questions to answer."

"You're not helping, Dom."

"I'm doing all I can, Harry. Tell me why all the hurry?"

Harry takes a long draught of tea and closes his eyes. Dom is not going to like this. "It's Curly," he says at last. "We think she's using. Strike that - we know she is."

Dom isn't sure whether to be astounded or outraged. "What? You think she's doing drugs?"

"–No, Dom. I'm not saying we think it – I'm saying we *know* it. Coke mostly, but some tablets too. She's not a hardcore addict, but who's saying where these habits can go. At the minute, it's just enough to give her a lift at the weekend and get her down again when it's over."

"–No way. It's a mistake. It has to be. Listen Harry, I spend quite a bit of time with Curly – more than anyone else. And yes, I know the stories, but that's all a long time ago."

"–I'm sorry, Dom, but we have her on tape."

"What? How?"

But the words aren't even out of Dom's mouth before he works out the answer. They have a wire in Fatman's car. It's so easy; it's their property anyway. They probably have them in all the cars to help them keep tabs on their troops.

"No – not your BMW," says Harry reading his next thought. "You're in and out of a police station every day so there's too much chance of someone finding it. And besides, Dom, I really do trust you. That's not to say your other bosses aren't doing it..."

"But, it doesn't make sense. Curly is the one who's always forcing me to go to meetings for the gambling."

"Transference, maybe? Look, there's a few signs to look out for. Red eyes, runny nose, loss of appetite – money going missing..."

They both laugh. It is a well known gag in the Hurley family that any cash lying, either secreted or openly, in any room in which Curly finds herself is hers and hers alone. But neither man laughs for long.

"Seriously though," says Harry, "you can't be surprised. You know that Curly likes to live close to the edge."

"–Given her upbringing, I think she's remarkably normal. Her father is a crooked cop and her uncle, well no offence, Harry, is you. But as for her being a little out there, I'm seeing that less and less now we're together."

"You mean you have a calming effect on her?"

"I do. I really do."

"Trust me, son, that's not you – that's the Ecstasy. Will you check her out?"

"Spy on my girlfriend, you mean?"

"Look, if we find out she's getting her stuff from Fatman, well, let's just say it changes the picture entirely."

"I don't want to hear this, Harry. In fact, I can't hear this. Come on – you're the man who insists on it. I have to stay clean. And besides, you don't do that anymore. Let the police bust him and we'll all take our chances."

"You'll never catch him. You're not good enough. And nothing we have is usable."

"Will you let us put our own tap in the car? A police one?"

"Never going to happen. Far too dangerous a precedent. You'll have to get another way in."

"Okay then. How about I go and talk to Eamonn McBreen up in CID? He's very discreet."

"Hmm. Anything to Charlie McBreen? My father's old cellmate? God rest them both."

"Son and heir of the same."

"Lord, what's the world coming too? Yes, you can talk to him. But that loud rattling noise you can hear is two very unhappy old skeletons turning around in their coffins down in the cemetery."

*

Dom is far too astute to confront Curly directly. Instead, Harry persuades him to leave a small pill-box of Diazepam in his jacket, where she's bound to find it on her morning trawl through his pockets for lunch money. And sure enough, by the time Dom gets out of bed, it's no longer there.

So later that morning he takes the lift to visit McBreen in CID and asks him can they get some form of trace on Fatman.

"Drugs?" asks McBreen.

"You hearing stuff?"

"We hear everything," grins the older man.

"Will you do something so?"

"Sounds like you have a personal interest there, Detective Dunne?"

"What do you mean by that?"

"You know full well what I mean by that. How do you think I know about Fatman?"

Dom closes his eyes and says a silent prayer as he realises they're watching his girlfriend. McBreen, though, is not a bad sort and throws his colleague a bone.

"We can't bust him, though," he tells Dom.

"I don't follow. Why not?"

"You're a bright lad, Dominic. You work it out. Suffice to say, I'm not officially privy to any of this. In fact, there is a directive that it can't come near my desk or anyone linked to Harold Hurley MP. You get what I'm telling you...?"

*

"Oh Christ," says Harry when Dom fills him in over lunch at the Culturlann. "They're running Fatman..."

"Per-sackly," agrees Dom. But the old joke fails to raise even the smallest smile.

Harry sighs. "It's what we get for paying a minimum wage. Socialism's great in theory – but it'll never buy you a holiday in Disneyland. There are only two reasons people do anything in this world – love and money. And, as you know, money is the only one that abides."

Dom laughs at Harry's tacit rejection of 100 years of party policy. But it gives him an idea.

"This guy now has three salaries – one from you, one from us in the cops and one from his sales. Maybe we should target his assets."

"How? He's working for you, remember."

"What about non-payment of tax? As I always say, if it's good enough for Capone...The Inland Revenue will take his house, his car and all his bank accounts. And he can hardly blame it on you."

"How much has he?"

"McBreen reckons one mill plus change."

"I'm in the wrong business – that's ten years of my salary."

"Yeah. But where can he spend it?"

Harry knows well how hazardous it is to show cash and smiles: "Shame the Revenue has to get it all. I don't suppose there's any way..."

"–Don't finish that sentence. No. Absolutely not."

"Okay. Okay. What's the latest on Curly?"

"She's not doing anything, Harry. She's clean. Period. I'm one hundred percent sure."

"Jesus, you are blind. Listen, Dom, I have a new tape of her asking Fatman for an eightball of Cathal and ten Doves for the weekend..."

"–'Cathal'?"

"Yeah. Irish for Charlie..."

"Ah, I have you. But listen, she's in my apartment all the time now. Unless she has a built-in secret compartment somewhere about her body that I don't know about, she's not using. And her car's clean as well."

"You sure?"

"I search it at least once a day, when she's at work. And I have to say, I'm not liking this surveillance on her one bit at all."

"Suck it up, son. You'll be doing it for the next fifty years, with the grace of God. But remember this, Dominic, as soon as we catch her, it's over for her. Straight out the door – and a long spell in rehab to boot. Or, if she decides to fight us, jail. We can't ever show favour to our own. It's bad for morale."

"I understand completely – and I'll be sure to pass on your kind regards and sympathies to your niece. So, what about the tax-man?"

"I'm not sure. We start involving him in our affairs, and you never know where it'll lead. Let me check with our, ah, treasurers, and get back to you."

"Put all your little mice in order first?"

"Don't get cute. Those little mice pay for guys like you to go to Oxford."

*

All is quiet on the Fatman front for ten days after that, largely because Curly is away on an Assembly trade mission to the Far East, selling her home city as a centre of software excellence. It's her first trip abroad since hooking up with Dom, but she experiences a considerable damper on her return when her boyfriend meets her at City of Derry Airport.

"You have to meet Harry in the morning," Dom tells her. "He's going to sack you."

"Over Fatman?"

"In one."

"What are you telling him?"

"That he's wrong."

"Doesn't he know I'm going to sort it out myself? My own way?"

"He does not."

"And why not?"

"Because this is information which he is better hearing after the fact. Now, tell me I am wrong..."

"You are not."

*

The next morning, Curly, as is her wont, tells Harry he can stuff his meeting where Fatman stuffs his stash, then switches off her phone so he can't track her.

But at midday, Dom gets a text to come urgently to Harry's office at the Jack Kennedy Inn, so he zooms over in his Beamer as fast as his penalty points will allow him. And who is sitting in the leather armchair opposite his uncle only Fatman O'Fallon. And he does not look pleased. Not one bit.

"I want my money back, Dominic," he growls. "And I want it

now."

"I have no idea what you're talking about," replies the detective. "What's this about, Harry?"

Harry shoots Dom a look which comes in about halfway between utter animosity and grudging respect, then points to the large black ministerial briefcase on the table.

"Self-raising flour," he smiles. "Or at least 99 percent of it is. Perhaps, one percent cocaine. Or so Fatman tells me. Apparently, he only ever gets to taste the one percent..."

Dom pulls a confused face. "I still don't get it. Why am I here? Does Fatman want me to arrest someone for selling him fake drugs?"

Fatman, however, is not there to dance and gets right to his point. "I want my one point two million pounds sterling, cash, back from your girlfriend, and if I don't get it, I'm going to bring the whole house down."

Harry holds up a silencing hand to Fatman and turns to Dom: "You're not the only one who's expecting a present back from Thailand. It seems your girlfriend and Fatman have this arrangement, but that Curly is after welching on her end of the deal. After pocketing all of Fatman's money, needless to say."

Dom nods sympathetically. "Well, as you and I know all too well, Harry, that is her form. But I'm not sure there's anything I can do. It sounds like it's a matter for the two of them."

Fatman moves quickly for a big guy and makes a dive up out his seat, going for Dominic's throat. "Don't kid yourself, Dom. I'm going to make it all about you – and big Harry too."

But Dom, who is a senior footballer in a not-so-distant life, drops his shoulder and allows Fatman to clasp fresh air, before volleying him in the join. Fatman gasps dramatically before falling to his knees on the carpet in front of Dom.

"Actually, Fatman, you're the only one this is about," Dom tells him. "I'm after playing my friends in CID a tape of you attempting to intimidate an honest, hardworking Assembly woman, into carrying drugs across international borders. Clear as day you are telling her how you will blow the whistle on her fifty-quid a week Coke and Ecstasy habit – which as you'll realise by now is a total put-up job to suck you in – unless she flies you home a case of Bangkok Bunga Bunga. Oh, and by the by, Ms Gilmore is most happy to undergo a drugs test to prove she never uses the stuff."

Fatman is down on his knees but not out. "I'll go to the papers. I'll tell them all about Harry."

"Actually, you won't. Even CID are smart enough to realise that any information, however sordid, you may have on Uncle Harry is now sufficiently tainted as to be totally useless. In fact, CID are so embarrassed by this affair, that Eamonn McBreen is to take over all their business in Derry tomorrow – and your two former handlers are being re-assigned to Animal Welfare. And yes, there may be a little in-joke there - who says the cops don't do irony? So, in short, if you go to the papers, you will go to jail for trafficking – and you will spend fifteen years in Maghaberry Prison or as long as it takes one of your dissident cousins to work out that you're a tout. And, I have to confess, there are some people who may even tell them...Some people even in this room perhaps."

"You bastard."

"Alternatively," says Dom putting his hand inside his jacket pocket, "you can take the twenty thousand pounds I have in this envelope and disappear out of sight for ever. But before you leave, you will head into the media room downstairs and give us a full video-confession of all your crimes and of how you are lying about Harry to CID all these years. Just in case you ever change your mind..."

"And if I don't? What if I decide to stick it out here?"

But Fatman can't keep it up and all three men start to laugh, if a little sheepishly.

"Good luck in your new life," Harry tells him. "Next time, don't be so greedy. Oh, and never underestimate a young woman with a pretend drug habit."

Fatman takes the envelope and nods sadly. "Don't worry, Harry. I won't. And Dominic – well played, son."

*

Unusually, Harry decides to forego his lunchtime walk and instead suggests to Dom that they eat in his office. After all, there is only so much exercise one heart can take in a day. So, they order up two prosciutto baguettes garnished with sun dried tomatoes and olive oil – and a couple of celebratory beer.

"So," says Harry crunching off about three inches of bread and meat, "what's she going to do with all the money?"

"What money?" asks Dom.

"Fatman's one point two million minus expenses."

"Oh yes. Well, that's not really your concern, Harry. She's no longer your employee – I mean, you're only after telling me this morning that you're sacking her for conduct unbecoming."

"–You can't be serious. I'm the guy who…"

"Look, we're all winners here. You no longer have to worry about Fatman, the town is rid of its biggest dealer, and I'm now walking around with CID's severed genitalia in my pocket."

"–And Curly gets herself a villa in Tuscany?"

"A ranch more like it. It's a good time to be buying."

Harry grins what-the-hell and raises his Bud. "To my niece," he laughs.

"And my new fiancée," replies Dom.

Harry blinks twice. "You serious?" he grins.

"Absolutely."

"You poor sod."

"Actually, Harry," says Dom, "I am many things. But poor is no longer one of them."

An Ordinary Derry Mother

For Anna P, A True Hero

T he shooting dead of Clack-Clack Cleary in his mother's home – while mindless, merciless and very, very gory – is, if we're to be honest, no surprise to anyone who knows the little bastard. For Clack-Clack, who originally gets the name after his double kneecap replacement, is a longstanding lowlife of the highest order.

Among other arts, he is an expert in thievery, intimidation and playing both sides against the middle. But he also has a cowardly streak as wide as his big fat mouth, and he tends to save his worst excesses for women.

Two former Mrs Clearys-to-be are on the record as saying that Clack-Clack has a predilection for producing Stanley knives and holding them to their throats if they don't bring the beer and nachos quickly enough. One of these ladies, however, is a distant cousin of Harry Hurley, which, as you'll gather, is how Clack-Clack winds up getting his new kneecaps in the first place. Though that is back in the days when such admonishments are socially acceptable. And they can never happen now that Harry the Hurler is a statesman up at Stormont Parliament and also MP for North Derry.

Anyhow, the day after Clack-Clack gets clacked for good, Harry rings his nephew Dominic, a trainee detective at Derry's Strand Road PSNI station, and invites him for a summer stroll in Ness Woods to give him a little off-the-record briefing. This meeting is not strictly protocol – hence the private meeting-place – but Harry is always anxious to advise his nephew on sensitive matters such as violent gunplay. And Dom is a dutiful protégé who values both Harry's high-level input and the most beneficial effect it has on his fledgling career.

Harry is standing tapping his watch when Dom zooms into the carpark, two minutes late.

'Sorry,' Dom says, banging the door of his roadster. 'It's all just kicking off back at the station. I'm lucky to be here at all.'

'Is Clack-Clack's old ma after confessing?' suggests Harry.

'You're a witch,' laughs Dom, pointing at Harry's iPhone. 'Is the word out already?'

Harry sighs and shakes his head. 'No. It just makes complete sense, that's all. No-one else I'm talking to wants him dead – at least to that extent. Ten years ago? There'll be a queue, and I'll be right at the top of the line myself. Even five years ago, you'll get quite a few takers. But now? Things are just too sensitive.'

The two men double click the electronic locks on their cars to be sure then amble into the woods, towards the waterfall and Shane's Leap.

Harry picks up a pebble and flings it absent-mindedly in the direction of the gushing river. 'What's the story, so?'

Dom sucks in a mouthful of fresh woodland air and closes his eyes as he rewinds to the beginning. 'Well,' he says, 'Clack-Clack is back living in his mother's house this last year now since his missus gets that court order. But recently he's starting to pick on his youngest sister Bella, a lovely wee thing who's putting her nursing studies on hold to look after her mother - Mamma C has only about six months left, the doctors tell us.

'Two nights ago, Clack-Clack has a full charge in him and, when Bella tells him to keep it down, their mother's trying to sleep, he starts slapping his sister around the kitchen. But Clack-Clack doesn't know his own strength and knocks Bella clean out. So Mamma hears the ruckus, comes down the stairs and goes straight for the shed where she roots out old Pappy's shotgun. Then she comes back into the kitchen and, from a distance of two feet, or best we can tell, blows Clack-Clack's head clean off his shoulders.

'No word of a lie, his left ear winds up in the budgie cage – and Polly manages to eat about half of it before Forensics arrive.'

Harry grins momentarily. Like Dom, he loves the little details. But he quickly turns serious again as he remembers the bigger picture: 'There are no lengths to which parents will go to protect their children. You have no direct experience in this area, Dom, unlike myself. Though I imagine it won't be long if Curly has her way.'

'–Why? What's she saying?'

'Nothing at all. Just my little joke. And anyway, it doesn't matter if she's not taking the pill, so long as you're practicing the rhythm method...'

'You're an evil man, Harry.'

Harry laughs. There are few perks to being Curly's uncle, but messing with Dom's head is one of them. 'Anyhow, fathers and mothers will go to any extreme for their children. It's a genetic thing – they can't help it. Take Shane's Leap there for example.'

Dom pauses and looks at the thirty-foot gap over the top of Ulster's largest waterfall. Legend has it that the outlaw Shane O'Neill jumps this very gap centuries ago to escape from an angry mob. Indeed, it says so on the info-sign right outside the park.

'What about it?'

'Well,' says Harry, 'what's not always reported is that Mr O'Neill is actually fleeing the father of his teenage girlfriend when he makes this leap. The father, like all good fathers do, is attempting to dispatch his daughter's boyfriend to a horrible death on the rocks fifty feet below. Lucky for young Shane he is such a good long-jumper.'

'And your point?'

'My point is, never underestimate a parent's love for a child. It is just like the old song: "As long as you're living, my baby you'll be."'

'I don't know it.'

'Don't worry – you will. And if you've any doubts about what I'm saying, just think back on the story of Anna Phelan, and you'll know immediately what I mean.'

'Anna Phelan? I don't think I know her.'

'Then listen up,' says Harry, 'because you are about to learn something very important.'

Anna Phelan, a tiny, elfin widow-woman from the Brandywell, is perhaps, Harry's one true hero. Though curiously Dom is ignorant of the fact, up to this point. So, he pulls a couple of apples out of his man-bag, hands one to his uncle and asks for the story.

'Who is this lady – and why is she special then?'

Harry, who always likes to eat when he is speaking – to make it harder for other guys to record and re-edit him – chomps down on the Cox's Pippin and begins.

'What you're about to hear is one hundred percent true,' he insists, 'and not some shaggy dog tale dressed up as a short story. Anna Phelan is an ordinary Derry mother, with no huge education; getting on a little, and otherwise unremarkable other than she is probably the smartest and most determined person on the planet.'

Anna, says Harry, has this son, Patrick, who is the sun, moon and stars to her. Harry knows him slightly. Back in the late seventies, Patrick – whom everyone calls 'Hessy' after his uncle Heslin - is a republican soldier. And he winds up in jail for a long stretch after he and a pal are badly compromised. Hessy actually ends up with the better end of that deal, as his poor friend is shot and left to die on the street. Hessy, incidentally, has his chance to run, but instead he takes his pal to the hospital, where he's arrested.

After he gets out of prison, Anna decides that Hessy needs a clean break. So she arranges for him to visit his sister in America, and sure enough he loves it. After a while, he sets up a little business in New York, painting houses. And from what we hear, he is never happier. He has a bit of money; enough for a decent apartment, a car and a few beers at the weekend. Some of his friends will tell you that he can get a little mischievous when he has a couple in him – but there's no harm in him at all. He has a good, good soul – even the priest thinks so.

He's a big kid at heart too. This one week, he rings old Anna back in Derry full of excitement to tell her he's going to buy a new motorbike. He's going to join a bike club and tour America. Old Anna tells him to be careful, but Hessy just laughs and tells her he'll pick her up at the airport on it when she's coming out to see him in a couple of months time.

But the reunion never happens. Instead, just a couple of days later, Anna is getting ready for Mass when the local priest comes to the door with terrible news. Heslin is dead – from a gunshot wound to the eye. And within about five minutes, the New York papers are describing poor Hessy as 'alcoholic and depressive' and pointing the finger towards suicide.

The official story has it that Hessy spends this entire day drinking with his buddies in the Oak Bar in the Bronx, before this cop, who is dating the barmaid, takes him across the road to her apartment to sleep it off. This apparently is standard operating procedure for a lot of the ex-pat Derry connection who use the bar as a second home. But according to the cop, when he puts him down in a bedroom, Hessy snatches the gun off his belt, sticks it into his own face and pulls the trigger before he can stop him.

All of which is fine, except that Anna, and Hessy's friends in New York, know that it is also total horseshit. For a start, Hessy is five foot four and carrying a skinful – the cop is six-plus and stone-cold sober. But more importantly again, there are suggestions starting to emerge that this cop is no angel.

Unsurprisingly, despite the persistence of a group of Irish campaigners, the New York authorities decide not to prosecute the cop. And there is little anybody can do, as there is no money in fighting City Hall. Indeed, it is whispered that some of the cop's friends on the Force are starting to make life very difficult for anyone who continues to challenge the official version. And it looks like it's all over – except no-one is reckoning on the determination of a Derry mother.

Harry's story is interrupted at the point by Dominic's phone, which begins playing the theme tune from 'Hawaii Five-O'. It's Curly's personal ring-tone, and always gives the lads at the station a chuckle at Dom's expense, as he is not allowed to de-program it.

Harry nods his assent, realising the call will be germane, and Dom presses the Answer key.

'There's a couple of developments in the Clack-Clack case,' says Curly, by way of hello.

'Do tell, *principessa mia*,' grins Dom, knowing this'll be good.

'First, and most importantly, I must tell you I am now Mamma Cleary's lawyer. In fact, I'm in the station cells here this past two hours talking to Mamma, while you're upstairs talking to your bosses about what to tell Harry.'

'So that *is* your car over in the corner of the carpark? And there's me thinking you're back stalking me again. Well, that's good news for Mamma. A very smart move.'

'Yeah. But not such good news for you. I'm going to produce proof positive that the affair is nothing more than a messy suicide – and that you guys are after making a whole barrel of wrong assumptions and banging up a terminally-ill old woman.'

Dom takes a beat. 'That indeed will not look good on my score card. But I think you are discounting the fingerprints which I'm pretty certain are on the gun – plus Mamma Cleary's own confession.'

'The confession, as you call it, is nothing more than a Catholic mother trying to absolve her son from stigma of a suicide verdict. And the shotgun, it seems, is now missing from the evidence room, thanks to your idiot colleagues, otherwise I will prove within thirty seconds that it is in fact Clack-Clack who blows his own head off.'

'The shotgun's missing? That's not possible.'

'Yeah – the superintendent is hunting through the station evidence rooms like a maniac. Dozy article. He's sure it's in there somewhere, but he just can't find it.'

'So, what about Mamma?'

'If she's not out of here in ten minutes, I'm going to sue everyone in the building.'

'Thank God, I'm miles away enjoying a walk with my uncle. Keep me posted'

'We'll be home long before you *mi'amore*.'

'I know you will. *Ciao, ciao*.'

While the waterfall at Shane's Leap is, according to Mills and Boon, one of the 200 most romantic places in the islands, Dom can think of prettier people to share it with than Harry the Hurler. So, after he switches off his phone, he nods towards the path, and the two men proceed with their three-mile circuit through the woods.

Dom is keen to hear more about Anna Phelan – and how she tries to prove her son's death in New York is no suicide. And, given the day that is in it, Harry is just as keen to fill him in.

'When she hears the NYPD are closing their files,' says Harry, 'Anna boards a plane from Ireland and lands in New York, where she talks to Hessy's friends, who tell her lots of things about the case she does not know.

'A couple of days later, she makes her way to the NYPD headquarters, where she manages to talk to a sympathetic chief in a nice suit. She puts her evidence to the chief – including her certain-fact knowledge that her son is not depressive. But it is no use. We are terribly sorry, Mrs Phelan, says the suit, but there is nothing more we can do. The investigation is over, and our man is cleaner than a Mormon's teeth. Or words to that effect.'

Anna has better luck with the Medical Examiner's offices, however, and manages to persuade them to review Hessy's files. And sure enough, after a second inspection, they decide there is no way that Hessy's bullet-wound is self-inflicted. It has to be at the hands of someone else, and there is only one other contender.

Buoyed by this, Anna manages to get New York District Attorney on the phone and asks him what he is doing to get justice for her son. Now the DA is also a decent soul and after chatting to this harmless old woman for a few minutes agrees to meet with her. (And again, I'm surmising here, says Harry.)

So Anna heads into downtown Manhattan, where halfway up a monster skyscraper she gets shown into an office as big as dancehall. She is naturally very nervous and about as far from her natural turf as she is ever likely to come.

The DA is very taken with Anna and, unusually, he is quite frank – figuring the least this little old lady deserves is the truth. He confirms off the record that the cop is a rotten egg – this is the second investigation involving him and death-by-firearms. The ballistics, the DA agrees, are all wrong too and don't match the cop's story – and besides, it is very, very unusual for someone to shoot themselves in the eye.

More worryingly again, says the DA, there is a story circulating regarding another Irishman who, it seems, is in the flat at the time of the shooting. This guy is an illegal immigrant, and our rotten cop knows him well – so well in fact, that he warns him not to give evidence. However, the DA is now aware, off the record, that Hessy and the cop are having an almighty row – and that Hessy is challenging the cop, just before there's a gunshot.

Well, Anna, while not entirely astounded, is a little taken aback by how much the DA knows. So she asks him why he doesn't just try the case and let the chips fall where they may. But, for different legal reasons, the DA isn't able to do that – and instead, he can only wish Mrs Phelan well and bid her a safe journey back to Ireland.

Except Anna doesn't go back to Ireland.

Instead, she takes a taxi to the door of one of New York's most influential papers and asks to speak to the editor. The editor is very interested in her story and particularly in what she tells him the DA says. But there is no way that he, and his paper, are going to go up against the might of the US government without any proof, other than hearsay. It is your word against theirs, and I'm sorry Mrs Phelan but you cannot win a firefight without bullets.

And it is at that point precisely at which the little Derry mother puts her hand into her pocket and produces the little tape-recorder she is after using to record her entire conversation with the Manhattan DA.

* * *

It takes about three years from this juncture, but the cop is eventually convicted of killing Hessy and sent to jail for a long, long time.

'Sometimes,' says Harry, 'we all have to play a little dirty to make sure of the right result.'

The walk around the woods complete, Dom and Harry make their way back to the carpark, before their journeys back into town. They stand looking over the roofs of their cars to say their goodbyes and enjoy another minute in the evening sun.

'You know of course,' says Harry, 'that you're being played by everyone on the Clack-Clack case?'

Dom is perturbed. 'What do you mean?'

'It's not a suicide.'

'Oh, sure. I know that much from the fact the gun is missing.'

'Nor is it Mamma Cleary.'

'What? You're wrong - it has to be. Curly is only pulling a sly one to keep her out of jail.'

'No. Though she is definitely pulling a sly one. Just think what I'm telling you all day here. A mother will do everything she can to protect her baby – it's genetics. And in this case, given that it's too late to protect her dead son, old Mamma is perhaps shielding someone else...'

'You mean her daughter? Bella?'

'It makes complete sense. Bella's the one getting the pounding from Clack-Clack.'

'But without the gun, there's no proof of anything...'

Harry gives his nephew a wolfish grin. 'Per-sackly. And given that you're never going to find the gun, and no-one is going to cry too many tears over Clack-Clack's demise, your bosses and the coroner will be ruling it a suicide before you log on for duty tomorrow morning.'

'So Bella just walks away?'

'You think she should go to jail?'

'No. Well, maybe. I'm not a vigilante. Quick query – you're never buying Mrs Cleary for it, are you?'

'Not for a minute. Her own son? It's just not in her. Sisters, however, are a tougher breed. Bottom line, Bella is an angel doing her best to keep her mother alive – Clack-Clack is the devil driving her into her grave.'

Dom laughs a little uncomfortably and moves to open his driver's door.

'I still have your golf bag in my boot from the last day,' says Harry. 'You want to take it with you now?'

'Good idea,' says Dom, even though he never plays with anyone other than his uncle.

Both men zap their electronic keys and Dom collects the clubs from Harry. But when Dom goes around to the back of his own car to put them inside, he is a little taken aback to see his trunk is not empty. Very unusually, Curly's new summer jacket – a Ralph Lauren number that comes in at about five hundred notes – is scrunched up in a heap inside.

As he picks up the coat to fold the creases out, a large metallic object falls from inside it and drops onto the ground, landing with a loud enough clang to alert Harry's attention. The two men stare, jaws dropping, at the shotgun lying on the ground.

Harry then looks hard at Dom for a full thirty seconds, not wanting to ask the question. But in the end, there is really no option.

'Looks like we're going back to the waterfall again,' says his nephew.

Harry nods. 'Indeed we are...Sometimes, my friend, we all have to play a little dirty to make sure of the right result.'

A Case of Spirits

For Peck Forager

H arry Hurley MP is a cautious man, so it's now almost forty years since he last goes strolling along the river on the Prehen-to-Strabane side. But when his nephew Dominic Dunne the detective calls to say he has some serious business in Bready – and that there's no-one looking to shoot him in these parts this fifteen years now – Harry pulls an old panama hat down over his face and drives the six miles out from Derry to the North Tyrone Riviera.

A little while past the other side of Bready village, Harry takes a right turn down a laneway in the direction of the riverbank and spots an old farmhouse strewn with police and yellow tape. Dom, who no longer has to pretend any more, is standing at the gate and waves his uncle a big hello.

'Park beside the hedge there, and we'll take a dander up the river', says Dom. 'I dearly need to clear my head.'

Harry nods sympathetically. 'Dead bodies?'

'No, but we have two brothers – bachelors in their seventies – who are critically ill. No obvious signs of trauma. But both of them seem to be going blind too. We're thinking gas of some sort – or maybe even poison'

'Foul play?'

'Possibly. Their older sister, who lives in a cottage about a hundred yards down the lane, is a nasty piece of work – and she's lying through her teeth to us.'

'How's that?'

'She keeps babbling on about it being an old curse that's hanging over her family for generations – and there's nothing anyone can do about it. So we can pack up our gear and get to hell off her land, as we're not going to find anything.'

'A curse – you're kidding?'

'No. Something to do with the hanging of a murderer two hundred and fifty years ago. Or a half-hanging, she reckons.'

Harry smiles. 'Half Hanged McNaughten?'

'The very man. You know about it?'

'Absolutely. It's a very famous story – a surprising gap in your education. I'll tell you about it on the walk. Spectacular view here – you normally never get to see this aspect of the river.'

'I know. The old lady says the eldest brother has an offer of two million to buy out their farm – it's only thirty-five acres. The developer reckons he can put up forty luxury riverbank homes and offload them at half a million each. But old Esau won't sell. And his brother, Jacob, agrees. It's an old Protestant primogeniture thing.'

'Ah, the responsibilities of being a firstborn son. I remember them all too well. And what does big sister think?'

'It's a no-brainer. If the two boys predecease her – she'll sell in the morning. They've no heirs.'

'Sounds like motive.'

'Maybe. But, she's almost eighty now. Why wait so long?'

'You going to bring her in?'

Dom pulls a pained face. 'Not my call. And, well, there's an issue or two.'

'Do tell.'

'A distant cousin is a superintendent, and also...'

'Also what?'

'Her lawyer's already on the way here – and, trust me, she is one tricky character to deal with.'

'Oh, God. It's not the same she-lawyer as I think it is?'

'Of course it is, or she is. Now, let's get moving before my fiancée lands to spoil our walk. It's only five miles from our house as the broom flies.'

A hundred yards later and they are standing on the rough riverbank path, watching two starlings practicing dive-bombs against a deep blue sky.

'What's that in the mud there,' says Harry pointing to a wreck of wooden planks on a sandbar a little upriver.

Dom grins. 'Looks like a poacher's raft. They're after the salmon. They use all sorts to go out on the river after them: tables, old doors – this one guy even has a specially-adapted wardrobe. The local bailiffs call him Mothballs.'

Harry clicks his fingers in delight. 'So that's why he gets 'Mothballs'! I'm after making myself a tenner.'

Dom shakes his head wryly. 'Don't tell me he sells his catch to the Jack Kennedy restaurant?'

'I don't know what you're talking about. Our salmon is flown in fresh from Canada. Anyhow, back to McNaughten – do you know Prehen House?'

'Not really. Just from the festivals.'

'Well, as you'll know then, it's probably the most beautiful house in Derry – a massive Georgian manse with a view of the Foyle as good as this one. It's there since the mid 1700s. The local MP, Andrew Knox, gets it built as a kickback present from an architect, for allocating him the job of designing Lifford Courthouse.'

'–Thank God MPs nowadays are so honest.'

'Yeah, yeah. Just like cops and lawyers. Anyhow, back when the house is just new, Knox has this teenage daughter – name of Mary Ann, who is very beautiful and a bit ditsy. And she falls for this upper-class rake John McNaughten, who's about twice her age. Think Charlie Sheen only with a musket and codpiece. A pal of her father's actually.'

'Very naughty.'

'That's only the start of it. You see McNaughten, like your good self, Dominic, is both a handsome devil and an avid card player. He's hugely popular in the town too. But again like yourself, he can't play poker worth a damn. So after he squanders his fortune, he hatches this plan to marry Mary Ann so he can spend all her father's money as well.'

'I take it Poppa Knox is not impressed at this proposal?'

'Not a jot. Indeed, he sends Mary Ann to the four corners of the earth to get her away from McNaughten. But our man is a first class stalker and finds her every time. Worse again, he even tricks her into going through with a sham marriage ceremony in a little chapel in Derry city-centre. Fake vicar, fake best man, the lot. There's a plaque somewhere on Shipquay Street commemorating it.'

Things come to a head one day, says Harry, when old Knox decides to take Mary Ann away to Dublin for good. She's tiring of McNaughten – so doesn't protest too much when Daddy packs her into the stagecoach and gallops her up the Strabane road.

Just outside Bready, however, John McNaughten and a couple of his cronies ambush the coach, with a view to kidnapping Mary Ann. But the coachman pulls a pistol from his side and wings McNaughten on the shoulder. McNaughten's sidekicks scarper away on their horses but our man has business to finish.

Now, there are two theories as to what happens next. The first is that McNaughten tries to shoot Andrew Knox and kills Mary Ann by mistake, or alternatively, he decides that if he can't have Mary Ann, no-one else can have her and he shoots her deliberately. Regardless, the poor girl ends up mortally wounded in the coach – and her father escapes and vows immediate vengeance on her killer.

Poppa Knox, however, soon hits a major snag. McNaughten, despite being a rogue and a rascal, is also a much-loved character around the diocese. And Knox is a politician and is not.

And as no-one is prepared to rat McNaughten out, he is able to hide in the locale with some impunity.

That is, of course, in the days before tracking devices and mobile phones, such as the one in Dominic's pocket summoning him back to the cordoned-off house immediately.

'We'll finish the story later,' sighs Harry. 'Who is it anyway?'

'It's the sergeant – Curly is just after landing, and they say I'm the best person to handle her.'

'And are you?'

'No. But I'm the only one brave enough to answer back.'

Curly is waiting for them at the gate, fanning herself with a copy of *Modern Bride* magazine to remind Dom who's in charge. 'I want you to release my client Ruth Speaklittle,' she says to him by way of hello. She then flashes a smile that she is saving up for him all day, and he knows he will always do whatever she tells him.

Curly turns to Harry, briefly considers reminding him that this case is absolutely none of his business and to get to hell, but she relents at the last minute and instead decides to tease him about his panama hat.

'Great disguise,' she smirks. 'Are they all out of trilbies and trench-coats down at the secret agent store?'

Harry doesn't lie down as quickly as his nephew. 'May I remind you Assemblywoman Gimore that you are contracted to be working for me today in Belfast, as an MLA? Indeed, best I recall you have a vote this afternoon.'

'I have a pair,' she sniffs. 'Besides, as you well know, I punch in my forty hours for you. And it is none of your business what I do in my spare time. Unless, that is, you want to start paying me what I'm worth.'

'Dead or alive,' quips Harry deadpan. And they all laugh. With Curly, you can push it up to a point, but there will only ever be one winner.

'Tell me about Miss Speaklittle,' says Dom. 'We have her down as a possible poisoner who's trying to dispose of her brothers and inherit the farm. What's she saying to you?'

Curly takes a breath, and unusually for her, looks a little embarrassed. 'Actually, she says it's all to do with an age-old family curse.'

Harry smiles. 'Half-hanged McNaughten?'

'One and the same. Ruth says she's trying to tell that handsome young policeman about it – God love her, I think she means you, Dom – but he just won't listen.'

Dom is exasperated. '–This damned curse again. Can you fill me in please? And be mindful that everything you say from this point out is liable to end up on the front page of the *Derry Standard*.'

Curly closes her eyes, fully mindful of what happens to even the best lawyers when they start invoking sorcery as a defence. 'Can we stay off the record for the minute?'

Dom nods okay. 'But remember, if you don't want us to take her in, I need a story I can give to my sergeant.'

Curly grins. All that matters is finding a story that fits. 'Well, I gather you know the background to the Knox killing. What you probably don't know, though, is that after John McNaughten kills Mary Ann he goes on the run. And apparently he hides out around here, in an old barn. He can't travel too far because of his bullet-wound. Now, everyone in the area knows exactly where he is, including possibly the local doctor, but no-one says a word – because they all love him. So old man Knox proposes a reward, and sure enough, one local bigmouth takes the bait. As they're coming to arrest him, McNaughten takes out his pistol and tries to kill himself – but the ball falls out of the muzzle and he only succeeds in setting the side of his head on fire with the wadding and powder. Leaves himself stone deaf.'

Dom gets it at last. 'So I take it the informer is an ancestor of the Speaklittles?'

'Per-sackly. I think the guy is called Falkender or maybe Falconer. But, he has no luck with his money ever after. And because of his treachery, all his offspring are born deaf, dumb or blind – that way, they can see no evil, hear no evil or speak no evil. And from that day to this, the family never mind anyone's business but their own. That's why they're now the "Speaklittles".'

'Seriously?'

'Well, there seems to be something to the story. Old Ruth says she has three or four cousins who can't hear or speak from birth. Her own father dies blind and so does her uncle. And now her two brothers are blind.'

Harry nods his agreement. 'I remember old Pop telling me this same story forty years ago – the only time I'm ever out these parts before.'

Dom has the feeling he is being double-tagged here, so he changes the subject to give himself time to think. 'What happens to McNaughten then?'

Harry takes this one. 'As I say, he is a very popular chap – so popular in fact that even when old Knox claps him in chains, no-one will hang him.'

'What about the local executioner?'

'He refuses too – maybe he's worried it'll harm his business. So old Knox has to resort to building his own gallows. But he makes a hash of it. And when they try to string McNaughten up, the noose snaps in two, leaving John Boy lying on the ground very much alive. Worse again for Knox, according to tradition, if a hangman's rope breaks, the lucky victim must be set free. And the crowd knows this and calls angrily for McNaughten's release. But McNaughten, who is racked with grief over the death of Mary Ann, announces he doesn't want to go down in history known as "Half-Hanged McNaughten", so he pulls another rope over his head and finishes the job himself...And yes, I am aware of the irony.'

Dom scratches his neck, like he always does when he's confused, before turning to his wife-to-be. 'So what you're saying, Curly, if I can sum up, is that want us to believe that a two-hundred and fifty year old ghost is after striking Ruth Speaklittle's brothers blind? Please tell me you're not back hitting the vodka-tonics at lunchtime?'

Curly lowers her eyes and mutters darkly about crazy clients. Then suddenly her face cracks into a wide grin.

'That's it!' she declares triumphantly. 'Does anyone else smell vinegar?'

'Actually, I do,' says Dom. 'The smell's driving me mad all day.'

'What are you talking about?' says Harry.

Curly laughs. 'Spirits,' she says. 'But the kind you get in bottles – not ghost stories. Bring old Ruth back into the drawing room, and give me five minutes with her. If I'm right, we'll all be out of here by teatime.'

Fifteen minutes later, and Curly, Dominic, Ruth, Harry and three detectives are standing in the basement of a large shed, which is invisible from the main farmhouse – and deliberately so. For, while the shed upstairs contains cattle, the bunker underneath contains one of the largest and most sophisticated *póitín* stills-cum-bottling-plants in all of Ireland – right down to the electronic labelling machine and the wireless internet.

'They do about two thousand bottles a week,' says Curly. 'They flavour it with pepper, package it up as Czech vodka and send it all over the country. They get four quid a bottle which leaves them a very handsome profit. And one of their most loyal customers, Harry, is your old nemesis, Switchblade Vic.'

Victor McLaughlin, who is Harry's lifelong enemy before peace breaks out, has a fleet of pubs across North Derry. The two men, however, are now on the same page on most issues and even share the occasional beer.

Dom eyes his uncle and starts to laugh. 'You can't decide, can you?'

'Decide what?'

'Whether to tip him off or not before we raid them.'

Harry shrugs sheepishly. 'Yeah – but I'll not be calling him. If this stuff is poison, you have to get it off the shelves. And you can't trust him to do it himself.'

Harry turns to Curly. 'Isn't this unethical of you, but? Turning in your own client.'

Curly shakes her head. 'Ruth has nothing to do with the operation. Never touches a drop. It's the brothers' little pension fund. The farm makes damn all, and, as you know, they're not supposed to sell the land. Pity though – it's really beautiful here and so private.'

'I agree,' says Dom. 'So peaceful – and not a crazy Hurley in sight. You're far enough from the city to be a light year away, but just eight minutes from the bridge in a decent car. One of these days, you and me, Curly, will find a bolt-hole like this.'

'If you can stand the smell of the vinegar,' smiles Harry.

'That's the telltale sign all right,' says Curly. 'It's from the processing. The bootleggers can hide just about everything except the scent. And on a tranquil day like today, it just hangs in the air. I remember my father talking about the smell of vinegar on a Donegal hill and him knowing that a *póitín* still was nearby.'

'I take it then that the old brothers enjoy sampling their own product?' asks Harry.

'According to Ruth, they split a bottle between them every night. Never a drop more. Except for last night, which is Esau's seventy-fifth birthday and they decide to risk a bottle each.'

'Not a good idea,' says Dom.

'Yeah,' says Curly, 'But boys will be boys – and so will elderly men.'

Harry looks over at Dom, who is studying the computer in the corner intently. 'What happens now?'

Dom grins. 'The Customs and Excise chaps come in with their axes and go all Elliot Ness on the hooch.'

'And the two old fellas?'

'They're being punished enough. If they ever come round they may get a smack on the wrist but no more than that.'

'What's their chances?'

'Well, thank God they have a high tolerance. Because, if the measurements on this computer are correct, they're really lucky not to be dead. Some of this stuff is 120 percent proof – it'll peel the paint right off your Mercedes!'

After that, all is quiet for about six weeks, until one day Harry gets a call from Dom to inquire if he wants to revisit their riverbank walk up outside Bready. It is a glorious sunny afternoon, the first day of new soccer season. And the crowds of Manchester United fans in the Jack Kennedy for the game are making Harry want to dig up the scullery floor. So instead, he hokes out his Panama hat and races up the A5 towards Strabane.

Like the last day, he parks his car close to the Speaklittle farm, where Dom is already waiting.

They walk quietly down towards the river, Harry knowing well that his nephew will get to the point when he's ready.

Then at the bend just before the bank, Harry notices a big new 'Sold' sign and points it out to his nephew. 'How about that,' he says. 'The old brothers aren't doing too well, I take it.'

Dom grins. 'On the contrary – they're both back on their feet. Full vision, the works.'

'Lucky boys.'

'Well, that's a matter of opinion.'

'So how come the farm is for sale?'

'Not the whole farm – just two acres.'

Harry stops chewing on his blade of grass and looks quizzically at his nephew. 'I don't follow. Who are they selling to?'

Dom grins again. 'To Curly. For keeping their sister out of jail.'

'I'm still at a loss.'

'Well, to cut to the chase, apparently old Ruth is a lot cleverer than she lets on. And she is able to recalibrate the computer to produce spirits which are three times stronger than the recommended dose.'

'Enough to take your eyes out.'

'Per-sackly. And she confesses as much to Curly, who, I understand, advises her strongly to keep her mouth shut – and in particular never to speak to me about it. No matter how pretty I am.

'So is Ruth trying to wreck the business, or just kill her brothers?'

'Neither, really. She only tampers with one crate. And it's just to teach her brothers a lesson – she's not meaning to harm them. They're drinking way too much of their own product – and they're not particularly nice to her, after all she does for them. Cooking, cleaning, hiding their still – the usual. So, when the brothers wake up from the world's worst hangover, they know exactly what is going on and send for her. She tells them she's too tired to look after them anymore. She wants to get herself a little flat somewhere down by the seaside and have a long overdue rest. So they agree to sell a riverbank plot of the farm to Curly and give Ruth the proceeds.'

'After she nearly poisons them? Why not just rat her out and let her spend her retirement in a nice warm jail cell?'

'Ah, but the Speaklittle's don't rat, Harry. And since the days of McNaughten, they always keep their own business in-house.'

Harry takes a beat to survey one of the most stunning views of the Foyle Valley – a view his nephew now owns. 'So how do you know all this?' he asks. 'I can't see Curly telling you.'

'Normally, no. But, I'm after making a great discovery. If you switch her normal 40 percent Smirnoff vodka, for a dose of old Esau's finest – she'll tell you pretty much anything you want to know.'

'You are a very dirty article, Dominic – and I'm very proud of you. I take it you're not using the 120 percent rocket fuel, though?'

'God no. I'm saving that for cleaning the drains... But just by the by, avoid the punch at our house-warming party.'

Die Like A Rat

Author's note: a standalone version of this story was first published in Belfast Noir (Akashic Noir, 2014)

With nine months of detective training under his belt, it takes quite a bit to make Dominic Dunne throw up his breakfast. But this is precisely what happens when he finds John Norway's weirdly-disfigured corpse in the Oxfordian's private swimming pool.

'Worst ever,' he tells his uncle Harry Hurler MP over lunch that day in the nearby Jack Kennedy Hotel. 'The autopsy will report that there are significant burn marks all over his face, forehead, neck and upper chest. But between you and me, it's a whole lot worse than that. Spotty John's head looks like someone is after par-boiling it then dipping it into a deep-fat frier. Smells like it too...and people wonder why I won't eat bacon.'

Harry, who is munching a BLT, stops to stare briefly at his sandwich then recommences happily. 'What I don't get, Dom,' he says, chatting as always through his food, 'is how Spotty John can afford to be a member in there in the first place. A court clerk like him earns what? Twenty-five grand a year? And I know he makes a bit on the side – maybe another fifteen. But a club like the Oxfordian will run you eight a year, easy. So why does a man voluntarily hand over a fifth of his income, particularly when – and I mean no disrespect to the dead here – John will need every red cent he has to pull any colour of a woman?'

'Good point. On his best day, John's too fuggly to play the 'before' guy in the Blitz Those Zits ad. Maybe he's expecting to come into some bigger money...'

Both men raise their eyebrows knowingly. 'It'll not do him much good where he's heading now,' grins Harry. 'So, what else do we know?'

'Well the burns are probably from scalding water. Steam, maybe. But he's clean as a whistle from the chest down, which means that whatever else, it's not down to the pool overheating. Otherwise we'll be looking at the full lobster effect. Oh, and there's no scalding in his throat or on the inside of his mouth.'

'So maybe it all goes down somewhere else and they dump him in the Oxfordian to wreck the trail...?'

'Except the strangest, strangest thing is, Harry, the burns aren't the cause of death.'

Harry knows Dom is toying with him, but he's damned if he can figure it out. 'How then? –Out with it.'

'Drowning – and yes, in the pool, according to the forensics guys at least.'

'So what are we talking about? Some form of torture first and then someone holds him under?'

Dom scratches his neck, a little perplexed. 'Possibly. Except there are no restraint marks on his arms legs or body. And there doesn't seem to be anyone else's DNA anywhere near him. Not a solitary atom. Truth is, we're completely bamboozled. Murder without a single clue - there'll be a serious pat in the back for whoever figures it out.'

Harry laughs. 'Next thing, you'll be telling me you've no idea just why Spotty John is so unlucky.'

Dom laughs in turn. 'No mystery there, I'm afraid. The little weasel is as dirty as a late-night film.'

As yet, there are no public competitions to decide these matters for definite, but it is a safe bet that Spotty John is the county's number one petty blackmailer. And it is an occupation for which he is ideally-placed, as his day-job at North Derry Magistrates Court gives him licence to put the bite on all manner of low-level criminals.

It works like this. For a small fee, John will make sure that a defendant's name and address are withheld from newspaper reporters, and hence their readers, to spare the client considerable public embarrassment. But if a client decides not to divest himself of this fee, he can guarantee that the juiciest insides of his files – including all the stuff never intended for the public domain – will be leaked to the tabloids before you can say 'vigilante mob'.

Now, Dominic is a bright lad, and he knows that there are very few people who will want to talk to the police about their relationship with a shakedown artist – even a dead one. Because the next question is: And what precisely are the goods that he has on you? But Curly Gilmore, Dom's lawyer fiancée and Harry's political heir, happens to be well-acquainted with Spotty John from the courts – and there is nothing in Derry that Curly does not hear. So, seeing as they are all currently at home in the Jack Kennedy building, Harry and Dom take the lift up to her constituency office three floors above.

'Kiddie fiddlers,' she announces, as they plonk themselves into the leather armchairs opposite her oak desk.

'Excuse me?' replies Harry, confused.

'Spotty John,' she continues. 'He's trying to shake down a couple of child abusers. Not my clients, I hasten to add, so I'm not talking out of school. Their names are being withheld from the papers by order of the judge – until the trial ends at least. And there's a decent chance they're going to beat the rap. But if the names leak out, the public will assume the worst, and they're ruined anyway – even if they don't go to jail.'

Dom nods that he has it. 'And I take it these particular gentlemen have a big amount to lose?'

'Per-sackly. An awful lot. And that's before the community retribution team comes a-calling.'

The room goes silent for a few seconds. This next part is never easy – particularly when you're dealing with a woman who never gives away anything for nothing. But Dom needs the names. 'Off the record...,' he starts.

Curly laughs. He of all people knows she doesn't do foreplay. It's all duck or no dinner with her. 'Billy Black and Sami Zucker,' she says straight out.

'Not the Billy Black?' interrupts Harry.

'Billy Hairless, one and the same,' says Curly. 'And yes, the Sami Zucker as well. And they're in it together, so I hear.'

Dom gives a low whistle. 'Jesus. Zucker's one of the five richest men in the county. And an old pal of yours if I'm right, Harry?'

'Not so much of a pal. More of an associate. I know him from the North Ulster Chamber of Commerce, that's all – he's chairman this year. But what's a hotelier and developer of his standing, doing with a ten-bob hood like Billy Hairless? Billy's only interests are running girls, drugs and hitmen.'

Curly raises her eyes at Harry adopting the moral high ground but decides to let it go. 'Apparently,' she says, 'Mr Zucker has been feeling very lonely since splitting with trophy wife number two. So Billy has a full time job finding, ah, volunteers, to fill the void.'

Dom raises a finger. 'And these volunteers are compensated?'

'Handsomely. Except now it appears that one of the girls is under the bar.'

This time Harry has a question. 'By much?'

'Three months or so. Not that it matters – vigilante mobs rarely stop to ask. Zucker claims he's absolutely certain she's twenty-one. He insists as much with Billy. He's over sixty himself and doesn't want the girls thinking he's creepy...'

Harry, who is a lot older than his companions, shudders. In the end, everyone is judged by the worst fifteen minutes of their life. 'Are the charges going to stick?'

Curly shrugs like she wishes she could do better. 'Forty-sixty. You know yourself, big money has a way of buying itself out of trouble.'

'But they have the girl's statement?'

Curly nods. 'And also one from Billy Hairless, who I hear, is no longer BFFs with Mr Zucker after a row over a sudden increase in the finder's fee.'

Harry closes his eyes. 'So Billy's at the blackmailing as well. Gets himself an underage girl who looks a bit older and finds himself a rich patsy. God, I'm so happy I'm married to Audrey.'

Curly smiles. 'I'll be sure and tell her. Anyhow, personally, I don't think the mud will stick. Ultimately it's down to the word of a teenage prostitute and an unconvicted serial killer against a man who has four different judges on speed dial. Though in saying that...'

She pauses to let the men salivate a little. But Dom is starting to tire of the game. 'You have something else?'

'I do indeed,' she laughs, ending the tease. 'According to his banker, who is a friend of mine, Zucker is after withdrawing two hundred thou – in cash – from his personal just ten days ago. And, from what I hear, this money has absolutely no tail. But you'll never guess, coincidentally, who's driving around in a brand new BMW since the start of the week?'

Dom knows the answer and is in no mood for Curly's smarty-pants act. It's very different when you get to see the burnt-out corpse up close. 'Yes,' he says, 'the car's still sitting outside the Oxfordian. And the keys are in the late John Norway's pockets, no doubt.'

Curly is oblivious to Dom's tone and charges on. 'You have it in one. Sami Zucker is no fool and a very powerful man. John, apparently, is very discreet this time – it's not just a matter of shaking down Sami on the court steps. From what I hear, the whole set-up is anonymous – via email and texts from throwaway phones. But when Spotty John zooms past in his new coupé, Sami puts two and two together and makes dirty thieving rat.'

That evening, as his shift is about to end, Dom gets a call from Harry, summonsing him for a quick drink in his office at the Jack Kennedy.

Dom is driving but, after checking his pockets for breath mints, opts for a Bud Light. His uncle has a driver so can fix himself a handmade brandy.

Harry then stretches out diagonally on his suite, resting his brogues on a mahogany coffee table that has more scratches than a thirty-year-old record. And when he looks up he is wearing his best worried look. 'Are you and Curly okay?'

Dom's antennae shoot up immediately, along with his other defences. When in doubt, ask questions. 'What do you mean?'

'Don't do this, Dom. You're my son, or as good as. You're anxious and annoyed at her, and it worries me. Even if she can't see it. Is it just this case, or is there more to it?'

Dom takes a deep breath. His uncle is paranormally insightful, even more than Curly. 'Yes, there are conflicts of interest...And not just on this case.'

'Go on.'

'Money for a start. I seriously think Curly believes the world is about to run out and that she has to grab every penny, pound and pearl necklace that she can get her hands on. And our wedding next summer seems to acting as a target date.'

'Sounds like she's acting out her abandonment issues. She doesn't feel worthy and has to bring as much she can to the bridal table. Make sure Daddy stays at home...'

'You might be right but I don't want it, and we don't need it.'

'I know you don't. You're a gambler; you'll happily risk it all on one turn of pitch-and-toss. She's different – she needs the security.'

Dom has no argument there. But there's more. 'It's also possible,' he says, 'that despite my better instincts I'm beginning to take my job seriously. I'm becoming a little, what's the word? Honest? Rigid?'

Harry laughs. 'And Curly's chosen path in life, effectively, is to undermine yours.'

'Precisely – or so it seems at present.'

'Maybe you need to slow things down a little? The work-life balance between the two of you will eventually sort itself out, but it does need time. Take an extra couple of years. You're both very young – still in your mid-twenties.'

'I'm not sure. Curly's very strong on the face of things – but you remember what she's like when's she flying solo. She can be very vulnerable if she doesn't have a plan; open to making stupid mistakes. And besides, I love her too much to hurt a hair on her head. I can never say no to her.'

'Hmmm,' says Harry. 'One day you may have to.'

Dom necks his bottle, savours the brief buzz that shoots through his head then stands up to go.

'One other thing,' says Harry. 'You have a private – i.e. totally off the record and unattributable - meeting with Sami Zucker at his offices at the Berkshire Hotel tomorrow morning. Wear a good suit – and see if you can persuade Curly to run an iron over the rest of you.'

'You think he can tell me anything?'

Harry grins. 'Can Dolly Parton hold a pencil with no hands? Of course he can. Now, go and come back with the full story for me.

'Will I wear a wire?'

'Absolutely – but remember this guy is very sharp. He's after taking quarter of a million off the cops across the water for wrongful arrest.

'What for?'

'Interesting case: a customer winds up dead in one of Sami's cheap motels. It turns out the heating vents are leaking gas, so they charge him with manslaughter.'

'Sounds fair enough.'

'But the dead guy has a medium-sized dose of cannabis in his system, which, according the judge, means it's his own fault for not waking up. So Sami is in the clear, and the PPS are down a quarter of million for damage to his reputation.'

Dom shakes his head in disgust. 'Which is exactly why I hate the law.'

Harry downs his brandy and reaches for the bottle again. 'And me.'

It's not every day you get to call on eighty million dollars, so the next morning Dom cracks open a new shirt and pulls on his good suit, which is still minty fresh from a wedding a couple of weeks earlier.

As he's getting into his car, he buzzes Harry on the mobile and checks if it's safe to fill him in on the overnight news.

'Shoot,' says his uncle. 'I'm on the can, so you have all morning.

What's happening?'

'What do you know about lap-dancing cages?'

'Not a thing. What are they?

'They're the big steel budgie cages they have in nightclubs - for those semi-naked dancers you pretend not to be looking at when your girlfriend's with you.'

'You're kidding? I really have to start going to clubs again.'

'I don't doubt it. Anyhow, my buddies on the search teams are after finding one in a garden adjoining the Oxfordian.'

'And?'

'And, according to our records, the same cage is missing almost a week now from the Lap it Up Emporium on Clinton Street...'

'—which just so happens to be on the lowest rung of Sami Zucker's property portfolio.'

'Per-sackly. Better again, there's a couple of thin bruises on John's shoulder which the pathologist reckons are there from him trying to bust his way out of the cage.'

'You mean you can lock them? Well, at least I know now what I want for my birthday.'

Dom snorts but mostly at the thought of what Audrey will say when he tells her. 'Also, we're after running a few checks on Spotty John's BMW and how he's financing it.'

'How much are we talking?'

'Thirty grand precisely, up front, plus his four-year-old Volvo. But here's the best part, the deal is cash only. And the car show-room still has a batch of the notes.'

Harry laughs. 'They don't happen to match the ones from Sami's secret two hundred grand stash, do they?'

'No. But they do match a bunch from a bureau-de-change that Billy Hairless operates in Dunavady.'

'So, Zucker cleans his money out in Dunavady. Good thinking. But God love Spotty John, the poor dead idiot. He's in way over his head.'

But Dom has more. 'I'm not finished - he's not in over his head at all.'

'I don't follow.'

'The Oxfordian pool, as I'm just after learning, is only four feet deep in the middle. Spotty John is five five So, whatever else, he doesn't go swimming out of his depth.'

'How does he drown so?'

'And that is the question everyone from the Chief Super down is asking this morning.'

Zucker's suite at the Berkshire takes up the entire second from top floor, and his personal office is about as big as Dom's last apartment and the one next door.

'Come in,' he says warmly, pointing towards a bar that looks like it's made out of cut glass. 'It's after one, so we can break open the gin.'

Dom demurs just unenthusiastically enough for his host to pour him a double and sits down into a leather couch, which is as comfortable as a mother's lap.

Up close, Sami is older and heavier than he looks on TV. His tightly cropped hair is Persil white, and his complexion is very pale, apart from a few brown liver spots on his hands. He's clearly investing a lot of money on his teeth though, which are permanently fixed into a shit-eating grin. He slumps down onto his E-Z-Boy, wipes an imaginary speck of dust off the trouser-leg of his five thousand dollar suit and raises his glass cheers. 'To happy endings,' he announces.

Dom reaches into my jacket pocket and pulls out a tape-recorder. But Zucker waves his hand no. 'Everything today is off the record.'

He then gestures to a door in the corner. 'That's the bathroom in there. Now, go in and take off the wire from around your waist, or I'll have four of my men come up here and do it for you.'

Dom toasts him with the glass, gets to my feet and heads for the corner.

'Your sergeant's a coward with a big mouth,' Zucker explains, answering the next question.

Ninety seconds later, Dom holds the wire aloft, pulls out the batteries and bows respectfully.

Zucker smiles again. 'Good. So, to business. For a start, I imagine you're wondering why the hell I'm talking to you at all?'

'Close enough.'

'Fact is, your people tell me you're a very bright man, Dom. And you and I could be useful to one another, not just today, but down the line.'

'I'm flattered.'

'Don't be. You have two great attributes, Dom. The first is that you hear everything, which is very useful for a man like myself in the business world, and the second is you say nothing, which is possibly more useful again. Oh, and you're also exactly smart enough to know your limitations, which means you never try to be too clever. And if there's one thing I have no time for, Dom, it is people who are too clever. Because you have to waste so much damn time watching them - and so much damn energy trying to out-think them, that it's easier in the long-run not to have them round you at all.'

'Would that include people like Billy Black?'

Zucker sighs and his face seems to sadden. 'Ah, the late lamented Billy Hairless...'

'What do you mean "late lamented"?'

'Are you saying it's not out yet?'

'What's not out?'

'Your colleagues in CID are after going to Billy's flat about an hour ago to question him about a horrific incident at the Ox-fordian. It seems some poor court clerk winds up dead there a few days back. But when the police jump in the door on Billy, he pulls a gun on them. And I'm afraid, after that there is only going to be one winner...'

Dom is staggered. 'Billy is dead?'

'As an old joke. And the malicious allegations which he is level-ling against many pillars of our society are dead along with him.' All of a sudden Zucker's dancing blue eyes are cold and grey. "From what I hear, the bullet hits him right in the middle of the forehead. Splits that big bald head open like a watermelon.'

He pauses, leans in and winks menacingly. 'Apparently, you can buy anything for ten grand. Only sorry I'm not there to see it for myself...'

Dom has to fight the urge to retch and finds his new shirt is sticking to his back with sweat.

'Anyway', says Zucker, the genial host again, 'Harry tells me I'll probably need you sometime down the line, so I'm now going do you a favour.'

Dom stands up and puts his drink on the table. 'I'm sorry, Mr Zucker. I'm not for sale.'

'Well in which case you can chalk one off the many I owe your uncle. But either way, you're not getting out the door, until you hear this story.'

Dom walks towards the door. Everything in life is a test.

'This is how it works, Dom: solve the Spotty John murder and you'll get your first stripe – maybe even a couple.'

'They're pretty sure it's down to Billy Hairless.'

'Yeah – but you don't know how. And it's important both you and the public at large do know how. Because then, everyone who ever gets to hear about my blackmailing problem will know how we deal with people who tell lies. And b, it will show that the police are perfectly correct to go into Billy's flat with all guns blazing.'

'You want me to help clear you of...?'

'I'm already in the clear – aren't you listening? The only witness against me is dead – the girl never wants any of this in the first place.'

Dom nods sadly, surmising that another ten grand is on its way there. 'And what does Harry think of this?'

'Harry is a twenty-percent share-holder in this hotel. If I sink, so does his chit. Why do you think you're here? It's always about the money, son.'

Dom is suddenly unable to move. He realises that if he leaves the room now, he has nowhere to go. But he's not for sitting down again, either.

Zucker starts talking quickly. 'It's simple. The cops are one hundred percent sure Billy is behind it. And there's no-one in the

press will doubt it either. Billy's an evil little sewer-dweller. He has the motive – and he has the form. Open and shut. Except...'
'Except what?'
'Well, it would be just perfect if Billy's involvement can be, ah, corroborated by the real story. If the truth can come out. It may distract prying eyes from the rest of the circus.'
'So you want me to frame Billy Hairless, posthumously?'
'Lord no. You won't be framing anyone. Billy is Spotty John's jury and executioner.'
'Don't you mean *judge*, jury and executioner?'
'Not exactly – but if it'll make you sleep better...'
There is a long pause while Dominic thinks. 'Only problem is, I've no idea how it all goes down.'
Zucker smiles. 'Good point. So listen up carefully.'

Four hours later, Dom finishes typing up his copy, and adds just one handwritten footnote: the source of the story will never be disclosed. He then emails it through to Chief Superintendent Mike Mortimer, according it security status 'H.F.C.', the in-house code for Highly Confidential.
The story begins forty years earlier, when Billy 'Hairless' Black is just a little child. A nasty-tempered brown rat takes up residence in the family's outside toilet – and refuses to leave or, indeed, eat Billy's mother's poisoned cheese. Old Pa Hairless, however, is a very resourceful man and builds a self-locking cage, which he laces with fresh chocolate. Sure enough, the rat gets himself trapped inside – and it is eight-year-old Billy Junior who gets the honour of disposing of the still-live rodent. So he takes the cage to a nearby ditch and attempts to submerge the rat in the water. The difficulty is that even when he takes the cage to the deepest part of the ditch, the rat is just big enough to stand up on his hind legs and get his nose above the plimsoll line. Then, however, Billy has a brainwave. He goes home and boils up a kettle on the stove. Half an hour later, a drowned rat with a burnt snout is floating toes up in the ditch.
Enticing Spotty John into the lap-dancing cage proves exactly as

easy. Billy Hairless knows his mark – all it takes is an open door and a fifty-pound note. They then take him from Lap It Up to the Oxfordian in a van, use John's own after-hours key to let themselves into the pool area before playing four rounds of boil the tea-urn. Security, it seems, are off on the sick.

'Sami Zucker reckons it is an entirely inefficient way to drown someone, by the way,' Dom tells Harry, when they meet up for their walking-lunch on the riverfront the next day.
'Why's that?'
'It takes about an hour or an hour-and-a-half to finish the job. And the rats tend to squeal an awful lot as they're going under.'
A chill shoots through Harry like someone is walking over his grave. 'I don't imagine Sami will be too worried though. He's still down the two hundred grand to pay off the shakedown – plus whatever Billy is into him for.'
Dom nods and munches on his Boursin bap. 'Another five – but luckily it's all in shares in the hotels. And you'll never guess what?'
'They revert to Sami after Billy's death?'
'Per-sackly. Billy's big mistake is thinking that he now owns Sami. Even sees himself as his protector – hence his willingness to do the job on Spotty John.'
'Showing the world that no-one gets to put the bite on this meal-ticket but me?'
'In a nut.'
They walk on towards the new peace-bridge quietly, munching on their baps and drinking over-priced water. As they reach the Guildhall and the turn for home, Harry averts his eyes towards the river and lowers his head slightly.
'I'm sorry, Dom. For, you know, letting Sami off the hook like that. He's as low, if not lower, than Billy Hairless. But...'
Dom smiles and taps his uncle's shoulder affectionately. 'I'm a grown man, Harry. In an ideal world, Sami will spend the rest of his life rotting in jail. But for the minute, at least, we can't touch him. Without Hairless, the evidence isn't there. But be sure and

switch your money into something else, and we'll get him the next time.'

'I will. And thanks for being so decent about all of this.'

'If there's one thing being a compulsive gambler teaches you is that there'll always be another game. And it's more than enough consolation to know that two other quite rotten individuals will no long be bothering the public at large.'

'So what about John's money, the one-fifty or so that's still missing after the car? Can Sami get that back too?'

'Very unlikely. He can't find it.'

'Can you?'

'I don't have to find it. I know where it is.'

Harry stops suddenly, looks out over the river again, then checks the path both ways. 'Curly has it,' he whispers. 'Doesn't she?'

'Of course she does.'

'Since when?'

'Since the day John turns up dead. Remember that conversation in her office?'

'Yes.'

'Well, what she omits from our chat is that she is in possession all along of a sealed letter from John Norway, which reads...'

'Don't tell me: "Open only in the event of my death"?'

'The very same.'

'And the cash?'

'In a hidden safe in his apartment, which she retrieves using a security code - also in the letter. John, it seems, would like Curly to ensure that the money goes to orphans.'

'Like Curly and you?'

'That's her reading of it. Except...'

'Except what?'

'Except I don't want anything to do with it – and further again I won't have anything to do with it...'

Harry closes his eyes sadly as he takes it all in. 'The line in the sand. And there's me thinking you'll have it out with me first...I'm really sorry. Can I help in anyway?'

Dom throws his wrapper and empty bottle into the bin and nods his head. 'You can indeed, Harry. I'm going to need a room at your hotel for a few weeks...'

'No problem.'

'And a bottle of decent brandy on the nightstand...'

'It's there already.'

'And I need you to tell me it's going to be all right.'

'It will. We write our own scripts in life, Dom, and yours has a happy ending. I promise you that, son.'

Bad Blood in Dunavady

Derry is a small town, particularly when you are at variance with your fiancée. So a couple of days after Dom the detective walks out on his bride-to-be Curly, Harry Hurley MP arranges for the young policeman to transfer twenty miles out the road to Dunavady. Just for a few weeks. He also fixes his nephew up with a new house about a two-minute walk from the station and assures him he still has a room at the hotel back in the city for days off. But, they both agree he is probably best to stay completely out of sight for a while. Given Curly's well-known proclivity for revenge and all.

Curly, true to form, is not coping well with the break-up. Or indeed quietly. And she is currently taking out her five stages of grief on everyone from the milkman to opposing counsel. Harry himself makes the error of suggesting that Dom has a point about Curly needing to curtail her thieving, and is very fortunate not now to be wearing a cut-glass ashtray as an ear implant. Thankfully, Curly is also drinking night and day, so she is seeing two of him when she throws.

The good news, as Harry somewhat jocosely tells his nephew in the car out to Dunavady, is that at least they don't have to worry about Curly internalising it. "Let her rant and rave for a few months and she'll come to your senses. Before you know it, you'll both be marching up the Cathedral aisle looking like a million dollars. And besides, you'll really love Dunavady – Tommy Bowtie will give you the tour when we arrive."

Dom stares incredulously at his uncle the driving seat. "Is any part of that last statement true?"

Harry laughs. "Of course. The part about Tommy showing you around is one hundred percent. He's waiting for us now at his law office on Liars Row."

"Liars Row?"

"Yeah. Up until five years ago, it's Drumbridge Avenue – but then a couple of politicians open up offices down from Tommy, and the locals start referring to it as Liars Row. Then some smarty-pants decides it'll be fun to make a motion at Council, so now it's official..."

They dump Dom's suitcase and a couple of boxes at his new home, a big redbrick town house completely unfurnished apart from a bed, a leather armchair, a coffee table and a satellite TV. "It's just perfect," says Dom, flicking through the sports channels. They then hop back into Harry's Merc – Dom's sawn-off Beamer is too small for the boxes – and head off to meet Tommy, who is sunning himself outside his office.

Besides being the town's only solicitor, Tommy is also chairman of the Dunavady Policing Partnership and, after a series of hand-shakes and catch-up stories, he has news for Dom.

"Our duty inspector is looking for a year off to write his book. Apparently, there is such a shortage of firsthand accounts of the Troubles that he feels obliged to write another one. But he's also too old and is looking to get out – I don't think he'll be back."

"So, what does that have to do with me?" asks Dom.

"Tag, you're it," grins Harry.

"No way...Sure I'm not even a sergeant at home."

"The board says it's a good fit," chips in Tommy. "You'll be acting up for the first twelve months – then you'll do the exam, and we'll make it permanent."

Dom glares at Harry. "Quote, unquote: 'It'll only be for a fort-night – one month tops.'"

Harry meets the gaze, hard eye to hard eye. "We need to get you up the ladder quickly, son. Quicker even than the fast-track can manage, and this is the best way of doing it."

"But..."

"She has to think it's forever, Dom. Otherwise, she'll torture and torture you until you come back."

If Dom knows one thing from his previous career as a poker

player, it is that he can never beat a stacked hand. And unlike in stud, draw, Southern Cross and all those other games he is no longer able to play, Dom is not in this instance able to slap the dealer in the mouth or even walk away from the table. So instead, he does what all good poker players do on these occasions and smiles like an angel as the knaves make a heap of his winnings. Never let the bastards know what you're thinking.

"Okay so," he says to Tommy, "tell me all I need to know about this place."

Dunavady is a small and beautiful country town, full of smart and friendly country people. The population of around 3,000 sustain themselves by farming hilly land and telling outrageous stories to credulous visitors. Though, unfortunately tourism is currently taking a terrible hit because of the new bypass, and the locals are finding it harder to make an honest crust. Which means that Dom is going to spend a lot of his time tackling the holy trinity of rural Irish crime – smuggling, thieving and recreational medicine.

Dunavady-ites tend to have good relations with their Derry neighbours – even if they do view them as a little too clever for their own good. So Tommy warns Dom to expect a little circumspection from the townsfolk until they get to knock a few edges off him. But they'll warm to him in the end.

The rules of the policing game here are simple: Dom rounds up the usual suspects at the weekend and presents them to the magistrate, Justice 'No Holds' Barr, who sits on Monday, and Tommy then does his best to get them off.

"I'll apprise you of the local characters, as they emerge," grins Tommy. "And trust me, that won't take long. By the time the first full moon is over, you will know them all."

"–Any current cases I need to know about? Or anything I need to keep an eye on, outside the box?"

"Nothing really. Well, one thing, maybe. But it's so bizarre, I'm sure you'll not want to waste any time on it."

"–I'm intrigued. Do tell."

"It's a strange story – pretty sure there's nothing in it. It's to do with my niece Tanya. She's a good-looking girl, some might even say striking, in her early twenties, a little wild but never out of control. Your typical single, white female with a head full of feathers. Anyhow, she's also a regular Saturday night fixture at the Castle Inn, at the top of the town. So, a couple of months ago, she's in there and starts hitting it off with a very charming fellow, name of Averty. They sit and have a couple of drinks and before long it's all she can do to keep her hands off him. He's clearly well off, good looking – if a little short – and, of all things, he works as a professional magician. So you can imagine the entertainment she's getting – him taking hankies out of her ears and all that...And yes, Tanya is not the brightest penny in the till. Anyhow, she's just on the point of inviting Mr Averty back to her flat to see if he wants to search her for any more hankies, when all of a sudden she wakes up in a ditch five miles out the Drumbridge Road..."

"Aha. Sounds like roofies."

"We're not so sure. The test for Rohypnol says no, though it's never completely conclusive."

"Drink then?"

"No. Never more than three or four vodkas over a night. Dumb and all as Tanya is, she knows she's way too gorgeous to get that drunk."

"Hm. So what are they police doing?"

"Nothing at all – we're not involving you. At least officially. We don't want to draw attention to it. Unofficially, Mike Mortimer is quietly having a man trawl through police databases to trace this Mr Averty. But so far, nothing at all."

"–Mike Mortimer? As in Superintendent Mortimer, my boss in Derry?"

"Yeah. I'm also his personal lawyer. Small world isn't it?"

"–It's a village posing as a planet. But why don't you want to draw attention to it? This guy sounds like a predator."

"Possibly. But then again, Doc Clancy says there's absolutely no marks on Tanya, apart from..."

"Apart from what?"

"Well, here's the kicker. Apart from two little puncture marks at the back of her neck."

"Needle marks, maybe?"

"No. Not needles. Think bigger"

"What then?"

"Well the doc reckons it's teeth – human teeth. And by sheer co-incidence, Tanya's blood count is also quite low."

Dom snorts, trying to suppress a laugh. "What – you're trying to tell me it's a vampire thing??"

"Yeah, I know. Really stupid. Far too many Dracula shows on TV these days. Even the doctors are believing in them. It's probably just a couple of nasty tick-bites and a spot of anaemia – plus a charge of vodka on an empty stomach. Which is why we're not going to talk about it any more. Okay?"

"Okay. You're the boss."

"Yes I am. Anyhow, you'll have a lot more to worry you about this weekend. There's a local derby between 'Vady and Drumbridge, so get down to the station and start swabbing out your cells."

"You're kidding, right?"

"If only. See you in the courthouse on Monday. If not before."

A week later, and Dom is well on the way to becoming a native. His handling of the traditional riot between the Vady and Bridge supporters – involving a decommissioned water cannon and a mobile slurry tank – wins him many friends across the community. For the first time in decades, there are no post-match fatalities, no windows broken or even property damaged. Indeed, No Holds the magistrate compliments Dom on the fact that it is not often that he gets to see so many of the accused still wearing the evidence when they stand before them. Though maybe next time, he can hose them under a cold tap before bringing them in. As Dom leaves the court, the local newspaper editor, a shrewd old gossip by the name of Pencil Jim Stevenson, approaches him and asks him for an interview – just to welcome to the borough and all. But Dom is mindful of Tommy's warning not to get to big too quickly, so he politely declines.

"I understand entirely," says Pencil Jim. "Don't want to come off like a star after getting one half-decent result."

"Per-sackly," laughs Dom. "I will do a piece after I'm here a few weeks – and I promise you'll get the story. In the meantime, why not let me buy you a coffee?"

In the Castle Cafe, Dom orders up tea and treacle scones while his new friend grabs a corner pew.

"Why 'Pencil Jim'?" he asks, sitting down the tray.

The editor laughs. "Unlike most reporters I always carry a pencil in my pocket. If you're outside at a rally or a football match and it starts to rain, pens won't write on damp paper. Pencils always do."

"Very intelligent."

"Necessity is the mother of invention, Dom – it rains occasionally out here, you know. It's a pity you're not doing the interview this week - Tommy's unhappy with one of the main stories, so I'm pulling it."

"Tommy tells you what to print?"

"Well, he's a sixty percent share-holder, so yes. Normally he stays out of things, but he's probably right in this instance."

"What's the problem?"

"I can't say..."

"Ah, go on. You'll get your interview next week..."

"Nice move, Dom. Are you really that curious?"

"Can't help myself. I always have to see the cards in the hole. It's the ruin of me."

"All right, so. But it's a silly thing."

"I'm all ears."

Pencil Jim pours another fill of tea into his cup and grins. "You're going to think this is asinine, but it appears we may have a vampire in Dunavady."

"A vampire? You're kidding."

"Nope. True as I'm sitting here. On Friday past, this very pretty woman – about twenty-five – comes into the office with a bandage on her neck. Wants to talk to me – won't speak to the reporters. It turns out she's a tourist from Cork up here on a cycling tour."

Dom puts down his cup slowly as he realises this is not Tommy's niece he is hearing about but someone else. But he is careful not to give away another single tell.

"So she sees a vampire swooping down from the Castle, is that it?"

Pencil Jim grins. "You don't have to have the answer for everything..."

"Apologies. You have to remember I'm a big city smartass."

"Granted. Anyhow, this lady, Lucy, is staying for a couple of nights with her gal-pal at the Black Tower Inn, out at Eagle's Glen, and this particular evening they decide to go down for a nightcap. They're in the bar, and they meet this very charming guy – a magician by trade, and they have a mighty time altogether, until it becomes evident that the guy only has eyes for Lucy. And Lucy for him. So, the pal, who is the essence of tact, feigns a couple of yawns and slopes off. And after another couple of drinks, the guy, Averty, mentions he has a room upstairs if Lucy would like to come up and see a few more tricks in private. Which she does."

Dom holds his hand up to interrupt. "Quick description of this chap?"

"Thin and short. Long dark hair, ebony-black eyes, very pale clear skin and a set of teeth an Osmond brother would kill for."

"Narrows it down – he can't be local with teeth like that."

"Watch it, Dom – that's two strikes now."

"My apologies. So what happens in the bedroom?"

"She has no idea. She wakes six hours later alone in the bed, getting an earful from an irate manager wondering what the hell's she doing in the spare room..."

"You mean the room isn't Averty's."

"Precisely. And they say you're slow... So when Lucy gets up, she feels very light-headed."

"Roofies?"

"Possibly – but by her own admission, there's no need for them.

She's not going up there to put rabbits into hats. And then, here's the kicker..."

"The bandage?"

"Yes. As she's talking to the manager, she starts scratching her neck and notices she has two lumps on it – like huge tick bites. So the Inn, who are starting to worry that something is not right here, call in Doc Clancy, who says he believes the marks are from teeth – and that Lucy is after losing a sizeable amount of blood."

"Get out."

"My reaction to Lucy exactly. But she persuades me to ring both old Clancy and the Inn, who confirm the story to the letter. And the Inn even give me a matching description of the now-departed Mr Averty."

"Clancy mention anything else? Any other cases perhaps?"

"No – the bare facts only."

"Any CCTV at the Inn?"

"Sadly, no. We don't go a bundle on your big city gadgets."

"Apologies again. I just find all this unbelievable. But why doesn't she come to me with it? Why go to a newspaper?"

"Think about it. Would you want to make an official report of this?"

"But why a paper then? It's the next best thing."

"Because she wants to let women know that this freak is out there. And I agree with her – right up until Tommy Bowtie reminds me that he owns three-fifths of the chair I am sitting in. Which is why I'm pulling the story."

"Incredible."

"Yeah. But for all that – I believe every word of it."

That night, after Dom goes home and sticks on the machine to filter out Curly's drunk-calls, he switches on his computer and starts doing a little research of his own. And what he finds there astounds him.

According to several reputable websites, North Derry is actually the inspiration for the most famous vampire of all time – Dracula. Eminent historians believe that the Dublin author Bram

Stoker bases his character on a medieval Derry magician Abhartach O Catháin who, legend has it, rises from the grave at night to drink the blood of his subjects. The name 'Dracula' comes from '*droch fhola*' – the Irish words for 'bad blood'. And 'Abhartach', as Dom knows from his days studying Irish 'A' Level, is pronounced 'Avertah' in English. It is also the Irish word for 'dwarf', and all witnesses describe the modern 'Averty' as remarkably small.

Curiouser again, as recently as fifteen years ago, a workman is badly injured when he attempts to cut down a thorn tree said to be arching over Abhartach's grave.

"I remember it well," says Pencil Jim, when Dom meets him the following day. "The chain saw refuses to work, and when eventually it does, it nearly cuts the hand off the fellow operating it, and the ground below him seems to drink up the blood."

"You're joking?"

"Not a bit. It's all in the paper – come in anytime and read the archive. There's a dozen more bizarre stories like that, all concerning the grave. You think it's connected to the attack on the Cork woman? It could be a great yarn for the paper."

"I'm one hundred percent certain it is. If you hold fire for just another couple of weeks, I'll give the full scoop. And trust me, this is the type of story you'll be able to sell directly onto the nationals. Maybe even bring in a few tourists into the borough."

Pencil Jim claps his hands in delight. "You're not going vampire-hunting, are you?"

Dom looks right back at him stony-faced. "You bet your last pencil I am."

By Dom's calculations, Mr Averty will reappear within the next couple of weeks – he makes a bet with himself, it'll be on the night of the next full moon. And sure enough, he is right.

The Sunday after the August full moon, he is sitting in his little office reading the papers, when a very beautiful copper-haired woman of about twenty-two comes into the all-but-empty station. She looks very nervous and disoriented – and Dom can spot that she is wearing a new bandage on her neck.

"Are you okay, Miss?" he asks, beckoning her into his private room.

"Yes, yes," she says, picking her way uncertainly through the open plan front office. "I'm just a little distracted. Doctor Clancy is after ordering me to come and see you."

"What's your name?"

"Mina – Mina Murray."

"Well, Mina-Mina Murray what can I do for you?"

She smiles shyly at his little joke, and Dom thinks to himself there are times he really loves his job. She is just his type.

"It's like this, Inspector..."

"–Dom."

"Okay, then Dom. It's the strangest story – and to be honest, I'm worried you're going to think I'm nuts."

"Let me tell you, after last night in here, you'll not even get in my top fifty."

"Well, it's like this... I'm in the Dolmen Arms last night, when I meet this very nice fellow. A magician of all things. And after a couple of drinks, we decide to go for a stroll up to Forest Park Point, ah, to get a look at the view in the moonlight..."

"I understand."

"And the next thing I know, I'm waking up in the middle of the woods, feeling totally drained and with these two bumps on the back of my neck. You want to see them?"

She points to the bandage.

"No, no. So what's the doctor saying?"

"Well this is the ridiculous part – he thinks that Averty, that's the name of my friend, is after biting me on the neck and drinking some of my blood. But I'm sure he's not the kind – he's far too much of a gentleman."

"What about a Rohypnol test?"

"Yes. But no results yet. Doctor Clancy seems sure it'll be negative... Here's a note from him – he says you will know exactly how to handle this. You don't really think there's anything in this vampire nonsense do you?"

Dom furrows his brow and strokes his chin. "I think we have a really serious situation here, Mina. And the last thing I want to do is cause any panic. But we also need to act quickly before this demon strikes again. I have the makings of a plan in my head. So I'm going to get Doc Clancy down here, along maybe with Tommy Bowtie the lawyer and Jim Stevenson from the paper, and we can decide where to go from here. Can I ask you to hang on for a little while? I'll be able to round them up very quickly."

"I'm happy to wait, Dom. I feel very safe here. And thank you. Really. Maybe when this is over, you'll let me make you a cake for coming to my rescue."

And with that Mina gives Dom a look that shoots a thrill through him. It's the first time he's felt a stir since walking out on Curly more than a month past.

Dom goes out to the kitchen to make a few calls and ten minutes later, Tommy, the Doc and Pencil Jim shuffle into the office together. They are about to sit down in the chairs in the outer office – but they are a chair short, so Dom points them towards the bigger of the cells. "Twelve spots in there – all vacant, thank God."

So he opens the cell with his keys and politely allows Tommy, the Doc, Jim and the beautiful Mina to enter before him. Then, as soon as they are inside, he slams the gate shut and locks it. With himself on the good side.

"You're all under arrest," he announces, with a triumphant grin.

"This is outrageous," counters Tommy. "What for?"

"Conspiring to waste police time. I'm after speaking to No Holds, and he says I can keep the four of you overnight here, and he'll process you in the morning."

Mina looks very confused at this stage and starts to fill up. "What's wrong, Dom? Does this mean you don't want my cake?"

Dom laughs. "Tell you what, Mina. You take off the bandage – and if there are two bite marks under it, I'll buy everyone in the town a cake. How's that?"

Mina bats her eyes worriedly, as if she's about to dissolve into floods of tears, drops her head low – and then raises it again. But this time she flashes him a wicked grin. "You clever sod. You're the first rookie ever to catch us."

Tommy also gives Dom a smile and tips an imaginary hat. "Now be a good fellow, Dom, and let us out of here."

Dom just shakes his head slow. "I'm afraid I can't do that. You see there are two reporters coming here, from the *London Times* and the *Guardian*, for the court tomorrow. They are intrigued at the huge lengths Dunavady people will go to, to attract tourists to the borough – and they believe this will make a great story for their feature pages. Oh, and vampire stories really sell papers, or so their newsdesks tell me."

Pencil Jim and Doc Clancy start to protest. "You can't be serious," says Jim. "We're pillars of the community."

"Let's face it Jim, you yourself are exactly one hair away from putting me on the front page of your paper promising to hunt down this mystery vampire. And making me the laughing stock of County Derry for the next twenty years. It's what you are aiming for from day one. So you can hardly cry foul when you wind up shooting yourself with your own gun."

Tommy nods sadly. Like Dom, he is also a poker player – and knows he cannot beat a stacked hand. "How much is No Holds going to fine us?"

"Not a whole pile – fifty dollars a man. He knows you have the best interests of the town at heart. Even if you are trying to ruin the life of an innocent young policeman."

Mina shoots him another look with those sharp green eyes. "Is there any way to keep my name out of this? I'm actually a teacher in my day job at Drumbridge Primary School – and it is not going to look good on my record."

Her three companions nod their agreement. Dom hesitates.

"Please," she says, batting the eyes again. "After all, it would never do for a policeman to take a convicted criminal out for dinner, now would it?"

"What makes you think I'm taking you out for dinner?"

She grins again. "Well, clearly I need saving – and also I hear you have a thing for bad girls."

Dom has no chance – and knows it. He purses his lips so as not to come off too keen, but can't hide the smile. "All right so," he says after a slow count of five. "Friday night – at the Dolmen Inn. Dress nice. And take off that bandage."

"You going to let me out now?"

"Not a chance. Now settle in, you're all here for the night. If you need to use the bathroom just rattle on the bars."

Dom then turns on his heels and heads across the corridor to his little office, where he slumps down heavily into his leather chair. He shuts his eyes, massages his brow and says his silent prayer. "Oh Lord. Not another one."

Act of Contrition

Author's note: a standalone version of this story was first published in the Derry News (Easter 2015)

T he big steel gate is opened and Harry ambles along the narrow walkway to the allocated spot. No-one else about; just the way Big H likes it.

"You're looking prosperous," starts his brother. Harry waits. "'You get any more prosperous-looking, you'll need a push-up bra."

Harry grins. He gets it. He's fat. Peace is too kind to the top men. "You working all week on that one?" he shoots back.

"Not much else to do in here."

Harry lowers his eyes contritely. Give me another reason not to sleep, you little bastard.

Harry Hurley, the MP for North Derry, visits his brother Jimmy every Monday when it's quiet. Left to his own devices, it would be a lot less often, but there's no escaping his mother's most enduring legacy – Catholic guilt: "Your big mouth got him into this, so your big mouth can go and keep him company."

Harry no longer subscribes to the old ways. Not publicly at least. Jimmy, despite being a decade younger, is a lot more hard line. And a lot more damaged. Fifteen years in a ten-by-six cell, your only company the ghosts of dead innocents, will do that to you. Even after he got out that last time, it was obvious he was never going to make it. His head was shot to pieces. Jimmy "No Jokes", the papers call him.

"I'll tell you why I'm here, Jim—"

"You're here, Harry, because old Bridget makes you come. Doesn't matter that she's dead these five years, you're terrified she's watching your every move."

"I know for a certain fact she is," laughs Harry. "It's worse than when she was alive. At least then, I can hang up the phone on her. But still, I've a bit of a story for you."

"The new inquiry?"

"Yeah."

"'Bout time. What do you hear, what do you say?"

Harry smiles at the line from *Angels With Dirty Faces*. "It's all over, Jimmy. I'm gonna die yella…"

Jimmy isn't good at receiving bad news; his friends know it, his family know it and the entire staff of C Wing know it. Indeed, it's precisely because of his volatile reaction to bad news that the prison wags got to rechristen their governor "No Teef" O'Keefe.

Harry's problem today is that the findings from the new inquiry are too late to make any difference to Jimmy. And he's going to resent this. So, explaining to him that the result matters a lot to other people is better done in instalments. Accordingly, the older Hurley decides to take himself off to the Little Boys Portakabin and let his brother compose himself.

It's all his fault, of course; taking him on the march in the first place.

"Let him come, Ma. He'll be safe with me."

"He's eight years old, Harry. What if there's trouble?"

"No-one's going to try anything. There'll be too many people there. And you're always saying yourself that Jimmy has more brains than any of us. I promise I'll look after him."

"The only thing you can look after is the tail of a skirt. No, Harry. It's no place for a child – especially one as soft as Jimmy. And that's the end of it."

Except it isn't.

Boys will be boys, and Harry helps Jimmy out the living-room window while Bridget is out at the coal-shed filling the scuttle.

The parade itself is very orderly: a few stirring songs, a rowdy chant or two, but good-natured and well-mannered. "Up to its arse in country schoolteachers," as one labour leader puts it.

The bother breaks out, as it usually does, close to Aggro Corner after the main body of the march has passed into the Bogside. But it's just the normal handbags. Half-bricks and rubber bullets. No live rounds – Christ, never with these crowds. In saying that, the soldiers look different. Tougher. Angrier. Eyes nervous and hopped-up.

For the first time, Harry finds himself worried. Not of the riot. That's more fun than chasing girls or drinking cider – and poses less risk of serious injury if you stick to the rules. No. Harry is scared of one thing and one thing only: what Jimmy will tell their mother when he gets home. So before he can see anything worth talking about, Harry gets a policeman's grip on his brother's upper arm and ushers him into Rossville Street, towards the sanctuary of Free Derry.

When the shooting starts behind them, he tells Jimmy not to panic, that the soldiers sometimes fire over the rioters' heads to disperse them. But to be sure, he pulls Jimmy into a doorway at the High Flats, then steers him up to the third-floor balcony so they can recce an escape-route below.

"Look," says Jimmy, suddenly giddy. "There's Coach – and he's got a pebble in his hand! Wait till Mammy hears."

Sure enough, Jimmy's mini-football coach – a long-haired, skinny youth of about eighteen – is standing on the pavement below them, his swollen fist concealing a small stone. The soldiers have little cause to worry, though. Harry and Coach both play for the same Saturday morning side, and Coach couldn't hit a toilet if he was sitting on it.

Harry curses — but quietly so his brother won't hear. When his mother works out what's happened, she'll tear him more holes than a ten-dollar suit. And work it out she will. As their father used to say, she's like a copper only prettier.

Harry's only hope is to find some way of distracting Jimmy. Maybe they might get lucky and meet some of his friends on the way home.

But it's a moot point. As Harry looks back down to the street, a soldier is after firing a live round through the centre of Coach's chest, leaving a hole in his back the size of a human heart.

Harry doesn't want to go to the first inquiry, but at Father Colum's insistence, he eventually agrees. Colum is fiercer than Bridget and firmly on her side. "You owe it to your brother, Harry. He can't sleep a wink. He sees blood on the footpath every time he closes his eyes. You need to show him that when good people like you tell the truth, the State will recognise its wrongs. God will always win through."

"You really believe that, Father?"

"I can do no other, son," replies the priest, surprisingly gentle. "It's the very essence of our faith. It is all that we have — and is all that we are. Trust me, the State will do the right thing and the world will make sense again for Jimmy. So make sure you do the right thing, too."

"Okay, Father. I'll hold fire on Plan B for the time being. Just tell Bridget to stop lamping me with the back of her hand every time I meet her in the hall."

As he expects, Harry gets a rough ride on the stand; it's his first time in a courtroom, and there's a lot at stake. But unlike his many subsequent appearances in the box, at least this time he's guaranteed to walk out the same door he comes in.

Eleven weeks later, Harry's doubts are vindicated. The judge, who is naturally under pressure to look after his own team, stops exactly one hair short of calling Harry, the world's press and hundreds of other eye-witnesses flat-out liars.

With impeccable logic, the man in the wig says that if there had been no march to begin with, then no-one would have died. Some of the shooting was reckless, sure, but this is what happens when soldiers come under fire first.

It is all stitched up neater than a bishop's corpse.

That same night, Harry Hurley calls at his manager's house to hand in his football boots and his captain's armband. He then visits Coach's grave, where he swallows his very last flagon of cider and heads home for a final night in his own bed.

The next morning, he takes himself to a cottage close to a gasworks and swears an oath with other serious men to get justice. Or possibly revenge. It is a grey area, and Harry has no more patience to worry about colours.

Eight years later, Jimmy takes the same oath, with his brother, who is now Harry "the Hurler" and the man running the show, sitting at the top table. But this time, Jimmy says not a word to his mother.

Back in God's world, Father Colum takes to the drink like his life is about to end. And after a time, he is proved right.

"You remember your first sabbatical?" Harry asks Jimmy when they resume. "Back when you were a greenhorn?"

"You never forget your first. A total fit-up job. 'Positive traces of explosives' my lilywhite ass. Did they think I was some two-bit amateur? My hands were red raw from scrubbing them with your old wire brush. Jesus, and the smell of turps from the wash-bucket in the shed? I get sick just thinking about it."

Harry chuckles unsympathetically. "You got eighteen lousy months. Let it go — you were hardly The Man in the Iron Mask. And besides, there's still six pounds of gelly lying under the bedroom floorboards, if they ever want to make an issue of it."

"Bet I could have beaten it on appeal. That confession would never stick."

"The second one will stick, though. The real one..."

The dig lands right on the money.

Jimmy fires up immediately. "You're a dirty bastard, Harry. You're lucky I don't go through you. You, of all people, know I'm never getting over that."

Jimmy doesn't need reminding that gelignite isn't the only thing on his hands. The thought is as painful today as it ever was, and it never leaves him. Seven years old, lying like an angel in her coffin, in a First Communion dress. All thanks to a mis-aligned grenade-launcher, a too-quick armoured car and a teen-aged grim reaper.

He handed himself in the next day. But as he often says himself, it was two days too late.

He takes a breath. "She forgives me now – the mother, I mean. Or so she claims. Not sure I can understand how."

"She's through the other side, Jim. Can't allow the bitterness to weigh her down any more. Comes a time you have to let these things go. And she knows you're sincere — taking fifteen years right on the chin like that, when you could just as easy have walked away, and no-one would have been any the wiser. Did you ever see the wee child since?"

"Not since that Easter."

Jimmy has episodes where he meets the little girl all grown-up and she sings lullabies to soothe him. One time, he even asked her to marry him. But thankfully, Doc Clancy is able to wean him off the cooking brandy and back onto the Librium, and the visions go back into hiding.

"It's not the old doll I need to absolve me," says Jimmy.

"You're right," says Harry. "But nor is it the girl."

"I know, I know. It's down to me now. But like Father Colum says, the hardest person to forgive is yourself."

"He also says you have to accept the things you cannot change, Jimmy."

"I'm not sure I'll ever have the serenity, Harry. I envy you your ability to park things and move on."

"Don't," laughs Harry. "Most of the time, I'm just storing up trouble for a later date."

Harry stands up and pats his pockets. "Here. I'm going to nip back to the Portakabin for a quick smoke. I can't risk some comedian with a camera-phone getting a shot of me, now I'm sitting on the Health Committee."

"It's hardly a secret. They still have that old newspaper photo of you standing with the cig in your mouth, in front of the burning building in Dublin."

The elder Hurley smirks. "'Harry the Hurler lights up an Embassy.' We have to take it down from the office wall every time our new pals come to visit. They mightn't appreciate it. God,

I miss those days. Simpler times – a lot easier to spot the bad guys."

"I still find them easy to spot."

"That's part of your problem, Jimmy. You can only see two colours..."

"—Do you think I want to be like this? You think it's easy being the voice of your conscience? You don't think I'd rather be back at Med School, scoring with drunk nurses?"

"I'm sorry. And you're right – you're the only one left who can keep me honest. Listen, I'll be back in a tick; you need a breather."

"That I do. But hurry, Harry. I can't wait to hear again how you're going to free Ireland by dismantling the system from inside."

Harry winces at the sarcasm but recognises when he's being let off. "How do you stop a politician from choking?" he asks.

"I don't know."

"Take your fist out of his mouth."

Jimmy laughs. The old ones are always funny. Even when they're no longer true.

Harry needs a breather as well. His greatest fear is that if you spend too much time with a crazy person, they'll start making sense.

Jimmy and his friends got so accustomed to the conflict they became dependent on it. But while Harry will never forget the war, he's also old enough to remember peace – and he knows which he prefers. So, every time Jimmy has a sabbatical or a brainstorm and is out of action, Harry uses the time wisely. Fishing and reading poetry. And thinking. Finding his own peace.

And it works for him. After almost 40 years in the business, Harry has no regrets and few apologies, apart from his weekly duty to his mother. Back before it turned serious, he had all the ambition of a drunken lout. But, as soon as he was called, he was too smart an operator, too disciplined an organiser and too charismatic a leader to become anything but himself. But, as the poet reminds him, he had little choice in the matter. That was

Heaven's part.

Harry also knows from the poet, though, that it's time to let his great hatred abate, before it maims him. Sadly, it's too late for Jimmy. His shelves hold too much history.

Jimmy knew nothing about the first peace talks – they didn't dare tell him. He was too unstable, and anyway he was in jail then, so he had no vote. More to the point, the odds were very much against a deal in the early days, so there was nothing to be gained by upsetting him. Negotiation is a dirty word in Jimmy's book, right alongside sell-out and surrender.

Harry himself was still a non-believer in the early stages and, despite the optics, remained so most of the way through. Cease-fires, permanent truces, agreements and coalition governments – he's there for all of them and each time gives them his blessing. Publicly at least. But when he closes his eyes at night, he, too, can see Coach lying on his back with a hole in his middle. And the old man in the wig and gown, slipping a gun into his cold, dead hand.

It's the small things that start making the difference for Harry. At one of the first private sitdowns, he remembers running out of cigarettes. His opposite number in the Savile Row suit, who up to then will only address Harry through the chair, pulls a packet out of his pocket and hands him one with a wink. "Go on, Harry. I'm not trying to kill you."

"Maybe this time, you're not," says Harry, snatching the smoke hungrily. "But technically, I'm now in breach of my job description."

"And what's that?"

"Burn everything English – except their cigarettes."

His adversary winks. "Next time, I'll bring a minor royal…"

And just for an instant they are on the same side.

As they leave that meeting, Harry, without thinking, motions to shake hands, but his opposite number shakes his head coldly. "I could never take that chance."

Next time, though, he has a christening gift for Harry's new grandchild – a Celtic scarf. An unexpected gesture, as Harry concedes, but not unappreciated.

"The first British team to win a European Cup," explains Savile Row.

"The first *Irish* team," Harry corrects him.

And they both laugh.

As the process persists, Harry's not beyond taking chances, himself – small acts of contrition: handwritten notes of thanks, the occasional pat on the shoulder, or a Mass card for a personal loss. In the old days, anyone getting a Mass card from Harry the Hurler would likely throw up his breakfast.

But it's hard for him to take any joy in the journey; the road is too long and the climate is too fraught. What began as a dream is now a day job. He's in a marriage of convenience; a partnership devoid of trust, kinship or friendship. And whether he's the groom with the barrel at his head, or the old fellow holding the sawn-off, he's never quite sure.

Jimmy, however, remains the ghost at the feast. The first day Harry takes his seat in government, Jimmy rings him from the prison phone. "They'll let me out next week if you vouch for me."

"Hmmm...how long if I don't?"

"Four more years – and I'll tell Bridget on you."

"Will you keep your nose clean?"

"Cleaner than your new Mercedes."

"Ouch."

"I'll do my best, Harry..."

But by now, Jimmy's best no longer tallies with what's best for Harry. And three years ago, Jimmy is coming out of the Credit Union with the parish savings, when a posse from Harry's new police force stop him and ask him to return the money immediately. And put down the Luger.

After that, there are no more chances for Jimmy No Jokes.

Harry continues on regardless, carrying rocks up the mountain and back down into the valley. But between his weekly breast-beating sessions with Jimmy on the one flank, and the icemen on the other, he often wonders what the point is.

Then, just last week, the guy in the Savile Row suit, who has no official title but is running the play from the other side for this past fifteen years, asks to see him. It's about Coach. The new tribunal is due to report within the month.

So Harry sticks on his going-out clothes and makes tracks for the "Coffee House", a big country manor, far from prying eyes, where they do their business undisturbed. And on this occasion, no-one is blowing any smoke in the air.

It's like they are meeting for the very first time. And Savile Row is, unusually, quite nervous. As Harry comes up to the table, the Englishman stands up awkwardly, looks him right in the face and extends a clean hand. Harry notices his host's relief when he meets the handshake warmly.

"I'm not good at this, Harry. But, on behalf of us all, I want to say I'm truly sorry about Coach and the others. The report will spell it out in full, but the short version is that it was completely on us, entirely on us, and not at all on you. We were wrong, and we need to make it right with you. It is to our eternal shame that this day was so long in coming, and we will never try to hide things like this again. It is unjust and unjustifiable. And I'm asking you now, please, to have the grace to forgive us."

The genuine humility of the speech knocks the breath out of Harry. They never talk to him like that. Like an equal.

As he gazes back at his friend, something long-forgotten stirs inside him. He remembers what it's like to listen to words that have no trapdoor. A pain in his back starts to disappear into the air, as if a weight is being lifted from him. And he realises that for the first time in his life, he doesn't have to keep his shoulders squared for a fight. Relief, regret, exhaustion and joy sweep over him, and he's having real trouble seeing through the water in his eyes. But today, this hard man doesn't care.

"Of course, I forgive you, my friend," he says quickly. "And thank you. I know too well it's the asking that's the hard part."

GARBHAN DOWNEY

Jimmy takes it better than before. These days, he just doesn't speak. Harry is used to his silences. It's like that these past three years now, since the robbery.

"We're doing the right thing, Jim. You need to trust me. I know you're upset that you'll not benefit from it yourself. But the rest of us have to move on."

Still nothing.

"There'll be no more white coffins, Jim. It's the one way to make sure."

This raises the expected hair. "Are you never going to let me off the hook for that? What about *our* sacrifice? We have plenty of our own graves too."

"Yes, we do. But bear in mind our friend from Sligo, Jimmy: 'Too long a sacrifice makes a stone of the heart.' And you're not on my hook any more. The only hook you're on now is your own."

"Go to hell, Harry."

"I'm trying really hard not to."

Harry can't leave it like this. "Same time next week?"

"Can you come a bit earlier? I'm getting the decorators in."

They both laugh. They will always be brothers. "I love you, Jimmy. See you then."

As he turns to go, Harry notices the wreath lying slightly to the right side, so he straightens it up, careful not to stand on the grave.

He kisses his hand then touches it to the cold granite stone, before taking one last look — *James Pearse Hurley, Loving Brother and Uncle, 1964 – 2007, 'What is it but nightfall?'*

Harry shoots his cuffs out of his jacket then ambles back along the narrow walkway and towards the big steel cemetery gate. As he crosses out into the carpark, he gives a final half-arm salute back towards the plot before pulling another smoke out of his pocket by way of cover.

"You're in there a long time, Harry," says Dom, his driver. "'You talking to someone?"

"No, no. No-one at all. Just doing a bit of thinking."

Harry doesn't believe in ghosts. Not publicly at least.

A Gentleman's Exit

Big Pete, God rest his gentle soul, was a great friend of Harry the Hurler. Back forty years ago, Pete was a hopeless drunk before he found the escape tunnel and switched over to helping other guys still looking for the hatch. And in time, he became a much-respected source of sound advice for all sorts of other people with problems. Even life and death problems, such as Harry had.

'When the rollies finally caught up with Pete a few weeks ago,' says Harry, 'a very large crowd of us, who had very good reason to be thankful for his life, took him to the City Cemetery to rest beside his wife. But as they were lowering him into the grave, a mobile phone slipped out of a gravedigger's inside jacket pocket under the coffin and into the hole. No-one really noticed, so the undertaker signalled to leave it go and get it later. But a few minutes later, just as the priest was commencing the final prayers, the digger's missus rang him to ask what he wanted for his lunch.'

Harry's nephew, Dominic, who is sitting in the passenger seat, has already heard the story from one of his men. But it is a good yarn, so he gives a little nudge to let his uncle know to go on.

'No way,' he says. 'How bad was it?'

'Bad as it gets,' says Harry. 'The ringtone was Johnny Cash – "I fell into a burning ring of fire"…'

Dominic gives it the appropriate snort of laughter. 'I take it the family were pretty shocked?'

'Indeed,' says Harry. 'The only way they'd have been more shocked is if Old Pete had gotten up and answered it himself.'

*

Harry the Hurler spends a lot of time in graveyards. They are, he says, the finest places in the world in which to focus the mind.

'For a man who generally prefers actions to words,' he says, 'I've actually done a lot of hard thinking in my time. I've also discovered that there are many locations that are predisposed to it to - holding cells, courthouses, churches, hospital rooms, safe houses, and so on. But the problem with all of those is that you're under pressure and are only looking for a quick fix. A graveyard, though, with its built-in finality, gives you the broader view.

'I used to do a lot of my thinking when I was gardening – it teaches you about seasons, and how to play a longer game. But with all the cutting, pruning, shaping and digging, you start to think that you've some control on what's coming next. That you're God of your world. A graveyard reminds you that oh no you're not – and that only one outcome, and one outcome alone, is certain.'

Dominic nods but says nothing. He personally suspects that the main reason Harry spends so much time among the headstones is that he is trying to make peace with his many ghosts. For fear they mightn't want him about them when it is his turn. But, of course, Dominic, who is one of the smartest young policemen on either side of the border and is very attached to this man who raised him, would never voice such an opinion out loud.

Today, the pair are heading to a little coastal church in Donegal, less than an hour from their home bases in sunny Derry. They are going there, ostensibly, to inspect the final resting place of a German pilot who washed up on the shore nearby after being shot down over the Irish Sea during the Emergency – which is what Harry still prefers to call World War Two. The pilot has finally been identified, seventy-five years on, thanks to a battery of military and DNA databases, and his family now want to make a small donation to the church by way of thank you for burying him. So Harry, whose father's cousin was the church sexton who made the little wooden coffin from fruit crates, dug the hole and then planted the pilot - all without tipping off the authorities, is there to make sure all is neat and tidy for the Germans' visit.

However, as Dom well knows, Harry's ostensible reasons for doing anything can be about as authentic as his hairline and new front teeth – so he relaxes back into the passenger seat of Harry's Mercedes estate waiting for the inevitable. It doesn't take long.

Roughly at the dividing line, between Derry and Donegal, just outside Muff village, where huge grey military barriers had divided the island for the quarter-century before the Peace, a lorry has broken down, causing a mile-long tailback. Dom is too young to remember when hour-long waits were the norm on this little winding road. But Harry is an old pro at the waiting game – indeed, on one occasion he was delayed for a full six months at a similar border crossing, after an eagle-eyed sergeant spotted his driving licence had a whole other name on it. Oh, and the car belonged a whole other person as well, who didn't recall that Harry had taken it out on loan. Though he did not wish to press charges.

'You remember how we opened up these roads after the Peace in 1994?' he asks his nephew. 'It was all over the news?'

'I was five,' says Dom. 'If it wasn't on the Powerpuff Girls or the Turtle Assassins, it didn't happen.'

Harry winces at the dig. 'For this died the sons of Eireann...'

He tries to appear disappointed. But it is all for the optics. Harry knows well Dom is playing him at his own game. Despite the fact Dom is an inspector in the North's new police service, everyone knows that Dom is Harry's best friend, confidant and heir apparent. The man who will one day take over everything. 'You cheeky pup, it was a big, big deal. And besides, it was the most fun we ever had. It was like a holiday for the troops after the war. A full month of R and R.'

'I saw some of the old videos,' says Dom. 'You call that R and R? From what I remember it was a bunch of fat old armchair rebels giving themselves heart attacks and strokes. You spent weeks digging up bollards and re-tarring dozens of old border lanes that had been blocked off by the army. That's when you weren't trying to tear down spy-posts with your bare hands and lump hammers.'

'You're missing the point,' says Harry. 'It was good clean whole-some entertainment. We would get a team of men in to move the dragons teeth – that's what the bollards were called; then the soldiers would come in and replace them an hour later with a big digger. Then we'd go out and take them away again, and the soldiers would watch, wait until we'd gone and then redo them. Real Tom and Jerry stuff – they were a cartoon too, smartarse.'

Dom shakes his head: 'Yeah, for this died the sons of Eireann, indeed.'

Harry laughs. Blown up by his own bomb, as his father would say. 'It was symbolic, you cynic. We were removing the fences of our oppressors to reunite the fourth green field with the rest of our land. And the new peace made it all possible – if we'd tried the same trick before the ceasefire, we'd have gotten filled with more holes than the Nama Report.'

Dom laughs. 'And then the other three green fields just wel-comed you back with open arms...'

Harry flicks his eyes skywards knowingly. As if to say Your Arse. Well, as much as you can flick anything with a frozen forehead. But then, he pauses silently for a few beats, as Dom notices often happens when he is about to move on from his pretext.

*

After a minute, Harry points out the window of the still-crawl-ing car to the sign welcoming people to Donegal and Free Ire-land. 'You know,' he says, 'the "Border Busting" campaign also provided us with the first main challenge to our ceasefire?'

'How's that?'

'Well, we knew rightly that the Brits were going to open the bor-der anyway. That was part of our deal. But they were pretending to drag their feet so as not to appear too eager to the general public. They didn't want to reward our previous bad behavior and so forth. But truth is, even the most hardline planters were happy to see the barricades gone. A lot of their farmers had land on both sides of the frontier dating back hundreds of years and it had become a nightmare crossing from one bit to the other – your cows had to go seven miles down the road and through a checkpoint if you wanted to take them to a milking shed a few hundred yards away across a field. So, as part of our discussions, the Brits privately agreed that they would open all the roads completely before Christmas. And this let us put on a bit of a show. Make a big play of pushing on the open door, if you will.'

'So why was there a problem?'

'Well, there was this one British colonel who just couldn't follow the script; he was one of those upper-class guys. Name of Farquhar, like the old Derry writer. He couldn't read the nuances of what was going on. It wasn't his fault – it was the way he'd been made. He was one of these people who needed clear lines – but could never read between them.'

'I don't follow.'

'Well, taking down the hard border was a game that we were always going to win. But of course the men in suits couldn't tell their men in green that; they had to keep them impervious. So Farquhar pressed on with his bounden duty to police the roads like they were his own private dominion. His troops arrested our men, seized our machines and shovels, and even roughed up a couple of cameramen. Eventually I got myself a meeting with him and told him to ease up and drink some happy juice. But he just said he wasn't go to hand over sovereignty of a British border to some jumped-up Irish street thug. He would sooner die first. Or rather I would... Now, I was a little shocked at this sort of threat, given how far we had all come in the previous years. But as far as he was concerned, he was the master here, and his word was law. I knew what was going on behind the scenes, though, so at the time I wrote it off as just a bitter loser letting off some steam. And I didn't really think any more of it.'

*

The queue of cars starts to move again, then stops suddenly, prompting a loud number of protesting horns. Not Harry's though. He is serenity itself – and instead just tweaks the window down a little notch to let in some warm summer air.

'Farquhar should have known something was wrong when his bosses didn't charge us with vandalism for opening the borders. Or when they caught two of our On the Runs who were helping us with the clearances and quietly let them go. But he missed the signs. And we, the bad articles that we were, played up on it a little – and stretched him and his men to the point where he was becoming demented. We ran dawn to dusk openings at every hole in the hedge along the three hundred mile border from here to Warrenpoint. And then, when his supreme commander told Farquhar that he had to rescind all previous orders and, not only ignore my men, but actually start opening the roads himself, officially, he snapped.'

'He hadn't seen it coming?'

'Not a chance. It wasn't in his programming. He was about fifty years old back then and had spent, I reckon, fourteen years at boarding school and another thirty in the army. And he just couldn't cope in a world where the rules could bend. That he couldn't control. So, he refused the order on the spot, resigned his commission and disappeared right off the map. Or so the story goes...'

Dom shakes his head in disbelief. 'Please tell me you didn't do what I think you did?'

Harry holds up his hand to tell Dom not to get excited. 'We didn't want to get involved at all. It wasn't our issue. And besides, we had settled our accounts at that stage, and all trading had ceased. The big problem came when your uncle Jimmy caught Farquhar in my garden, wearing a ski mask, and carrying a gun, a bayonet and three high-impact grenades in his side pockets.'

*

About forty-five minutes after clearing the traffic jam, they arrive at the little churchyard where the German pilot is buried. It is a beautifully-appointed little spot, a full mile from the nearest town, on a lush green hillside overlooking the Atlantic.

Harry points out towards a tiny little dot on the seascape under-neath a low-lying cloud. 'You see that island,' he says, 'during the Great Famine, there were more than a thousand people living there. It was one of the very few places in Ireland where there was no potato blight. A hoor of a place to get to – twelve miles out over treacherous sea - and the wind would cut a hole in your coat, but for all that it served a great purpose.'

'Anyone there now?' says Dom.

'The last of the locals moved out in the 1970s,' says Harry. 'Still a few buildings there – and as far as I know the electric still works.'

''You been out there?'

Harry pauses. 'Yes I have. Several times in fact.'

'Hiding out?'

'Not exactly.'

'Visiting friends then?'

'Not exactly.'

Then the light goes on suddenly in Dom's head. 'Jesus, no,' he says.

'You have it now,' says his uncle.

Dom nods solemnly taking it all in. It was like a Shakespearean drama. 'What happened?'

'Well, Farquhar needed to be stopped. We had no option. I've seen that driven, psychopathic look in people before. And while you can have all the compassion in the world, in the end it comes down to either him or you. And, at that particular time, it could not be me. I was holding too many cards. His pals knew he was broken, and they made it crystal clear to us that they would have no problem if he were never seen again. They even offered to do it for us. But they're such a crooked bunch – twisted as a cat's shite, as my Da used to say – you could never trust them. They'd pull his body out of the ground in twenty years time with a hole in his head and my fingerprints all over the bullet. So we took care of it ourselves. And told them nothing.'

'I take it Farquhar didn't want to go?'

'Actually, he did. He knew well his own lot were out looking for him too – but that they wouldn't even give him the option we were offering. He was too much of a liability to them. But equally, he also knew he wouldn't be able to rest until he'd gotten me. He needed us to stop him. I, and I personally, had become all that was wrong in his world and he needed to correct that. The switch in his head had gone, and there was no resetting it.

'So, we read our rulebook again and again, and we must have kicked around a dozen ideas. There was serious talk of an alternative solution of walling him into a room and leaving him there to die – Greek style – so that no drop of his blood would be spilt. But, in the end, we all agreed – him too – that that wasn't in keeping of the spirit of where we were at. So, your uncle Jimmy filled his motorboat with food and supplies and took Farquhar to a little homemade quay that still exists on the far side of that island over there. He leaves out the same sort of parcels – including lots of books - every month; and one of the Doc Clancy's goes out twice a year to check the Colonel's fitness. Jimmy also sorts out the diesel for the generator – and arranges any other repairs and such. We've left a couple of flares there too, in case of emergencies – sudden illness, power-cuts and so on.'

'Does he not want to come back?'

'Not at all. He's gotten used to it. Likes it even. Barely speaks to Jimmy or the doctors on their visits. Just reads his books, tidies his neat little cottage and tends to his neat little garden. You know the way no man is an island? Well, Farquhar is as close as you get. And you know what? As long as he leaves us alone, we're happy to let him at it.'

Dom is suddenly maudlin. 'That's a terrible way for a life to end up, for all that. No love, no hope, no-one to care about you or miss you when you're gone.'

Harry nods. The world is indeed a terrible place when you run out of friends – even if it is all your own fault. Harry remains silent for a minute, chewing on his lip and then answers.

'Once a year, I take a trip out and ask him the same question: do you want to come back? All you have to do is play nice, and we'll sort out the rest. But, Christ help the man, he's just too honest. He just can't give the guarantee. He's too broken. But he tells me not to worry because there is no better place on earth than an island to do your thinking.'

'So when are you seeing him next?'

'This afternoon – as soon as we're done here, in fact. And you're coming out with me, Dom. You're part of the play now.'

'Ah, don't be putting this on me too, Harry. I'm carrying a ton of stuff for you as it is.'

'I'm sorry, Dom, but you have to. You see, I've been trying to find a way to tell you for the last few weeks, but I'm not going to be able to come here this time next year.... You have to take over. I've got cancer, not the treatable type, and this is my final trip to the island. So just think of this as one last little job you'll have to look after for me.'

Dom's eyes immediately shift away from the horizon and lock onto Harry's. Both sets misting over. Uncle and nephew. Or rather, as it has really been, father and son.

Harry shakes his head and wraps the shattered boy in a tight bear hug. There is nothing either of them need say.

'So you'll come over?'

'Of course, I will,' says Dom. 'I have no option. That was just about the best guilt trip ever.'

'Couldn't resist it,' says Harry. He wipes his eyes quickly then points out down the hill towards a little dock.

'Jimmy's boat is all stocked up and ready to go. You row, I'll steer.' Dom smiles at the familiar old joke and discreetly thumbs the water out of his own eyes. 'Can I not use the engine?'

'We'll see. It's only twelve miles. I like to save the petrol for the way back. For when it's my turn to row.'

The End

LETTERS FROM DUBLIN

Author's note: this standalone story, an epilogue to Garbhan Downey's novel 'The American Envoy', appeared in the anthology 'Dublin: Ten Journeys, One Destination' (Irish Writers Exchange, 2010)

Acting US Ambassador Dave Schumann writes home to his father in Massachusetts

Ballsbridge
Dublin 4

Monday

Dear Pop

Dublin's very different to Derry. Far, far busier. A lot more Yanks to take care of, and a helluva lot more Irish to placate. Not unlike Boston in many ways; low-rise, green and sprawling, with rows of spectacular Georgian terraces in the center. A few rougher neighbourhoods too, naturally enough. But I'll fill you in on them later.

The ambassador's recall was a big surprise to him – almost as big as the one I got when I was asked to stand in for a few weeks. But that picture of the guy in the rubber gimp-suit with the foot-long attachment looks nothing like him, no matter how many affidavits the *Daily Dublin* says it's got.

Not that I should get too comfortable here. Billary warned me herself: "It's just until we can make a proper appointment – no offence…"

Why would I get offended? It's not as if I want to spend the next five years apologising for every American computer company that's shutting up shop and calling home its dollars.

We fund one in five jobs in Ireland, which was great when we were rich, way-too-busy and needed the help. They gave us pretty much carte blanche – a smart, lost-cost workforce, no unions worth a damn, little or no business tax in the middle of the Eurozone, and, to cap it all, they speak better English than we do. In short, we could crap all over them, just as long as we kept crapping money. Now, though, they've become expensive, so our corporate giants are hunting the world for newer and cheaper back alleys to crap over.

When I'm not listening to greasy little bagmen telling me their money's drying up, I'm spending my time sorting out the messes of US passport holders.

Take this morning for instance. One of our citizens walks into the cops on Pearse Street and tells the Guards (police) that he knocked down and killed a girl when he was a gap-year student here back in the late eighties. Full confession, apparently. Right down to where the body is buried.

Normally, we wouldn't get involved; it's a straight criminal matter. Except for two things. First, the confessant happens to be a Hollywood big-noise, who's currently in town shooting a movie. And secondly, the Guards are demanding his records from the States, but the geniuses at home are refusing to release them - probably on the grounds that he's such a well-known hell-raiser that the Irish will throw away the key. (You know this guy well, by the way. As do the rest of the world, so I'll just refer to him by the codename 'Champagne Charlie' in honour of his two lifelong pursuits).

The good news for me is that I'm now going to have to spend my entire afternoon in a cold prison cell, hand-holding an A-list prima donna, all the while trying to convince the Los Angeles DA, long distance, to forward details of the 160 crimes and misdemeanours that Champagne Charlie has committed since he graduated from the School of Soft Porn.

To add to the charm of it all, our client is still stinking drunk – and by stinking, I'm given to understand that he has committed the holy trinity of drinking transgressions – i.e. wet himself, puked all over himself and soiled himself as well. Not surprisingly, I'm now taking a quiet half-hour to drop you this note, while the station sergeant gets him another set of clothes. And a hose.

The good thing about Ireland, though, is that they're more close-mouthed about stuff like this. Charlie's in the chokey three hours already and not a word has leaked to the press. The stricter libel laws tend to slow things up as well. Back home, it'd be a front-page splash in *The Enquirer* before steam had finished rising from his pants.

Back in Derry, the biggest problem I'd ever have to face is whether to have a riverbank stroll with Ellie before or after a fresh salmon dinner at Da Vinci's. Oh yeah, and Ellie's just tickled pink that her new fiancé has blown town less than a month after promising her he'd never leave her behind ever, not even for the top job in London itself. (Irish women have great memories for detail.) Though she says she might come visit me at the weekend, if only to run a nail along the side of the company Daimler. I'll keep you posted.

So long and slán

Your loving son

David

* * *

Ballsbridge
Dublin 4

Tuesday

Dear Pop

Good news, bad news.

The good news is that our friend from Hollywood refused a film company lawyer and appointed our buddy from Derry, Tommy Bowtie, on my say-so. That keeps the movie people out of the loop, which will be very important when they start looking to cover their asses. They don't even know what he's coughed to – and we're sure as hell not going to tell them.

Naturally, they tried to outmuscle us by getting the studio-boss to ring head office in Washington. But Bowtie quickly convinced them to back off by warning them he'd release a few blood samples. And these, of course, strongly suggest that Charlie had been using Grade 1 narcotics during the entire filming process here – so violating about a hundred different insurance regulations, including the one that insists that our man gets tested each and every single time he goes on set.

Our other umbrella in the shitstorm was that I persuaded Ed O'Conway, who's now an Assistant Commissioner, to oversee the interrogation. This way, we've got a fighting chance that there'll be no leaks. Last time Ed caught one of his men passing papers to a journalist, he shut his fingers in a cabinet drawer so hard it actually sliced the top off his pinky. He then warned the guy, if he ever did it again, they'd play the same game in the restroom with the steel stall-doors. Only they would not be playing with fingers.

The bad news, though, is our client's head is full of jelly beans. He didn't say a coherent word during the two hours I was in with them yesterday. And today, he still looks and sounds like he's just been dragged out of an ER room. Eyes puffed up like a well-beat boxer, hair stiff with grease and jail-soap, skin the color of Grandma's corpse. No belly-fat though, despite his best efforts – but by my reckoning he's got a year tops before he gets his sandbags.

The only time he stops shaking is to wipe his nose on the back of his hand. And the little part of his brain that remains undamaged from years of partying is screaming so hard from withdrawal that we have to feed him half-tabs of calm-me-downs to get any sense out of him at all. And yes, these pills are of the fully-prescribed variety, but so help me, if I could get anything stronger and faster-acting, I'd serve them up to him on a spoon myself. The man is fried.

Bowtie finally gave in and let Ed's men question him this afternoon, for one hour only. Best we can tell, at this juncture, is that he was driving through Dublin city-center one night during this great smog they had in 1988, when a fair-haired girl of about seventeen staggered backwards out of a bar, right smack onto his hood. She flew straight over the car and thumped her head on the road, deader than an old joke.

He says it happened on Merrion Row or Baggot Street – not far from his dorms in Trinity College. He'd just left there to visit a pal in Donnybrook. He hadn't been drinking, he swears, though he may have been going "a little too hard" given the conditions. Because of the fog, there was very little traffic about, and no pedestrians, so "in a blind panic" he threw the girl into the trunk of his car and drove off again. He then drove around and around the city wondering what the hell to do, when it suddenly came to him that he could use the cover of the smog to bury her in Stephen's Green. This would be like their version of Boston Common, only a lot more secluded at night.

He borrowed a spade from his pal out in Donnybrook, telling him his room-mate at Trinity needed it to dig his car out of a ditch he'd driven into in Monkstown. And he headed back to town.

This, however, is where the fun part starts. The smog – which was caused by Dublin's myriad coal fires (long since outlawed) – was so dense that he got lost on the way back into the center. After about an hour though, he eventually saw a couple of landmarks he thought he recognised, and before long he was pulling his Ford Capri into a parking spot just outside an urban park. He hoisted the body over the railings very quickly - "she was just a light, little thing, man" – got his spade, and set to work. He buried her under about four feet of dirt, in the hollow middle of a thicket about ten yards from the fence.

Now at this point, Ed stopped the interview and quite reasonably suggested that they should all take a field-trip to Stephen's Green. To maybe recover the remains and put an end to the horror show. But the words were barely out of his mouth when Charlie announced: "Here's the thing, Mr O'Conway. I'm not sure I got the right park. Man, the smog was terrible..."

And of course, he started to cry again. So bad that Tommy called in the doc to give him a double dose of the there-there medicine. And we closed down proceedings for the day.

We've trawled the missing persons' files for the entire '80s but have turned up nothing so far. Ellie reckons the poor girl might have been an illegal from Eastern Europe. Though Ed reckons they didn't start coming this way until the early '90s.

Ellie says hello, by the way, and told me to advise you that your son is a lying, no-good shite-bag, (direct quote) who's lucky she's still speaking to him. It's her own little way of telling me she misses me. And you're right, Pop. She is far too good for me. She's taking a few days leave from the radio station to come down from Derry tomorrow and help me settle in.

Naturally, her reporter's instincts have been piqued by this nonsense as well. Yes, God help me, I told her... But I made it clear to her that this is all hush-hush and that a good wife should always mind her husband's business.

She then pointed out, with some feeling, that she is not my wife. Despite all her damned waiting. And despite all my damned promises. And when will I ever just clear two damned weeks of my schedule to make room for the most important damned person in my life...? And while we're at it, where's her goddamned diamond ring? (Except she didn't always use the word 'damned'.)

Boy, I just love feeding her straight lines. She heard me laughing, realised what I done and slammed down the phone so hard that my ear is still popping. There is nothing in life as hot as a bad-tempered, red-headed woman.

So long and slán
Your loving son
David

* * *

Ballsbridge
Dublin 4

Wednesday

Dear Pop

Curiouser and curiouser.

Our man was telling the truth about being sober. According to his Trinity roommate, he never touched a drop until his last week or two in Ireland. Not ever. His only interests were girls and films. But here's the kicker, he paid for his year here, and bought his Ford Capri, by smuggling booze down from the North.

Charlie shared his dorm with a guy called Jimmy Blakeson, who was president of the student body and got a free room from the university for the privilege. Blakeson is a consultant surgeon at the Mater Hospital now. And as healthy and lucid as our guy is a big ugly mess. Makes Charlie look like the picture in the attic.

Ed visited Blakeson at his office, rather than bringing him in. They're still treading very softly as, incredibly, the story hasn't broken. Tommy Bowtie has warned the film company that if anything spills from them, he'll release the blood tests and close them down permanently. And Bowtie still has the biggest mickey on the table, as they say over here.

Blakeson told Ed that our man never mentioned anything about his hit-and-run. Stuck up for him – said he was very careful driver. No surprise there. But the Doc was more than forthcoming about their regular jaunts into Newry, when the two of them used to fill the Ford Capri to breaking point with cases of whiskey - Powers and Bushmills. In those days, liquor in the North cost about half of what it sold for in the South. So there was money to be made, good money, if you could get it past the customs. Beer was cheaper again, though a lot harder to transport.

The boys sold their wares all the bars in Dublin 2, splitting the profit fifty-fifty with the publicans. And that's how Champagne Charlie, who Blakeson says wasn't a Champagne Charlie at all back then but really a sweet guy, paid for his sabbatical. Just one trip a week could net him three or four hundred clear; handy money in the eighties.

Blakeson himself never took a dime from the trips. He just went along for the rush. And anyway, Charlie took the real risks. It was his car that would have been seized. And he was the guy who charmed the cops and the customs men into waving him through checkpoints, time after time. Just gave them that warm Southern grin or maybe a little joke in that soft Texan accent. Cool as ice, too. Wouldn't have mattered if he'd had a crate of Semtex in his trunk. So damn plausible. Little wonder he made it big as an actor.

Blakeson did tell Ed a couple of useful things though. He revealed that Charlie was extremely athletic and strong, and once hoisted a full barrel of Guinness over a six-foot high fence, after a security man forgot to leave the gate unlocked. So a little thing like an eight-stone body would pose him few problems.

He also said our man had a steady girl for the last couple of months he was a student here. Name of Sue. Bit younger than him. Absolutely beautiful. He met her on Grafton Street, where she used to busk, singing Dylan on a jazz guitar. One day, after she'd finished her set, he went up and started talking to her and it was like something switched on in their heads at the same time. And that was that.

Blakeson couldn't remember her surname. But he said they were very serious. So serious that when he realised he was going to have to leave her behind, he started on the sauce. She was too young to go back to the States with him, and by the time he'd returned for a holiday the following year, she'd met someone else. Blakeson sometimes wonders if the missed opportunity wrecked his pal's life. He stayed in touch with him for about three more years until Charlie began making it large as an actor, and it became more and more difficult to get past his PA. Over the years, they arranged to meet twice when Charlie was filming in Ireland. But he blew Blakeson off at the last minute both times. So when his agent rang to say he wanted to meet him this time around, Blakeson didn't bother returning the call.

"He was a great guy then," Blakeson told Ed. "Even gave me his car as a going-away present. Made me promise I'd never drink when I was driving it. In case I hit someone. Maybe that was his guilty conscience. I don't know. I was delighted. It was such a big thing to have a car back then. And that very same day, I suddenly thought to myself, why the hell am I bothering with drink at all? And I've been that way ever since. Ironic isn't it? I quit the booze almost exactly the same time that Charlie started up. I know who got the better end of that deal."

For what it's worth, Blakeson finds it hard to accept Charlie was the type of guy to bury a body in the woods. Now, maybe – but back then, absolutely no. Last person in the world he'd have expected to become a lush.

The Guards, meantime, spent all day today conducting very discreet searches in Stephen's Green, using dogs and heat-seeking equipment and so on. But despite an extensive trawl, they found nothing apart from a wallet belonging to a government TD, who insists he was mugged a couple of weeks ago, and the condoms inside it aren't his.

Tomorrow, Ed's going to deploy a separate squad to Merrion Square, another fine Georgian park about half-a-mile from Stephen's Green, as it's just possible our man stashed the corpse there by mistake. Ellie reckons we'll have dug up half of Dublin by the time we're finished.

She landed in town this afternoon, by the way, and is currently out buying a pair of shoes for the supper we're throwing for some New York banker tonight. Very, very important - I've been instructed to kiss his ass until it bleeds money. It's her first gig as my official partner here, and she's solemnly promised not to swear, spit or play slap the capitalist in the mouth. Not that I'd mind, though. It would sure beat spending two hours discussing Keynesian macroeconomics.

We're placing bets on the number of times our guest says "fiscal rectitude". Any more than ten and Ellie has to pay me a forfeit. I'll not tell you what, though - you're too frail and easily-shocked. Which reminds me, I'd better go and tell the nightshift to knock off the CCTV before we get ourselves another case of Death By Camera. Accidentally forgot to wipe the tapes? Yeah,

and my butt smells of blue roses.
So long and slán
Your loving son
David

* * *

Ballsbridge
Dublin 4

Thursday

Dear Pop
We stuck a beanie hat and a pair of aviator sunglasses on our man and took him out to visit the two possible burial sites today. The three days off the happy juice has levelled out his thinking, and he's making a bit more sense. On the downside, Charlie now realises the scale of trouble he's in and is a lot more circumspect about what he's telling us.
Tommy Bowtie told me privately that he believes the guilt may have been eating at his client for years, causing him to drown himself in hooch. Something set him off that way, and no mistake.
The film people tried to hit us with a Habeas Corpus writ in closed session yesterday, arguing that the "unlawful detention" of one of their employees was costing them a hundred grand a day. They have still no idea why we're talking to him. Bowtie was ready for them though and released a statement to the Press Association last night, confirming that his client had admitted himself voluntarily into a Dublin facility which caters largely for substance abusers. Not a complete lie, nor even close to it – given the current crop of Charlie's current housemates.
The papers all had their splashes about him this morning, a couple even speculated he'd nearly OD'ed. But it's nothing our man hasn't seen before. When he heard on the car radio that he was being treated at the Mater for suspected liver failure, he

laughed out loud (if a little sheepishly).

At Stephen's Green, we spent two hours pushing back bushes, before Charlie announced that the railings looked a little lower than he remembered. He remembers it being a bit of stretch to get the body over. So we drove down to Merrion Square in the Hummer with the blacked-out windows and started the same palaver there. Again, he thought the fence was too low – but we walked him around and around, forcing him to point out possible spots.

There was a bit of excitement when he stated a thicket behind the recumbent statue of Wilde looked familiar to him, but predictably, it came up dry.

After another half-hour of this nonsense, I skipped out to have lunch with Ellie at Patrick Guilbaud's Restaurant, a hundred yards away, and bring her up to speed with the investigation. I had the Black Sole (very apt given my company, said Ellie), while she had the Mushroom Rizotto with Puntalette Pasta. Though when she saw my fish arriving, she was so impressed she nearly gave up vegetarianism on the spot. Instead, she treated herself to an extra forty-dollar dessert for being good. And yes, you read right. Forty Dollars.

Over coffee, I thanked her for being such an angel with our guests last night. They were shaping up to be the dullest couple I've ever met - and I've had dinner at the London Embassy - when Ellie started telling stories about life at a small-town radio station. (Like the time she asked one rough old bartender to stop saying "shit" live on air, only to be told, "But you say 'f***', 'c***', and 'b******' every time you come into my place..." By the end of the night, she had the banker laughing so hard that the Veuve Cliquot was running out of his nose and onto his red silk bowtie. Indeed, he laughed so hard he's going to build us a new IT factory in Dun Laoghaire.

We were staring out the window of Guilbaud's, holding hands and happy to be together again. And I was just about to produce the ring, when Ellie suddenly sat up straight, snapped her fingers and said, "I bet I know where the body's buried. Pay the check, and let's go."

We rushed on our jackets and headed down the steps onto Merrion Street – and she pointed down the road, directly across the road from the square.

I spotted the high railings she was indicating and closed my eyes in dread. Then I saw the copse ten yards behind the fence and knew immediately it was true...

America's top movie star had somehow killed a young girl and interred her in the gardens of Ireland's seat of parliament, Leinster House. And we were now going to have to ask the government for permission to dig up their front lawn.

My short but illustrious career as Ambassador Extraordinary and Plenipotentiary to the Republic of Ireland is about to come to an abrupt end.

See you soon – sooner than we thought.

So long and slán

Your loving son

David

* * *

Ballsbridge
Dublin 4

Friday

Dear Pop

What a difference a day makes.

It was Blakeson who started things, when he asked me could he visit his buddy last night. We decided to let them meet here, in the drawing room of the residence, and gave them a bit of privacy to catch up. Ed, of course, stuck a mike in the room. (Yes, another one.) And Tommy Bowtie had no objections, so long as he could hear what was being said as well.

Ed and Bowtie had been planning to come here anyway to discuss our campaign strategy, which boiled down to one single issue: should we tell the government what it is we're looking for? Yes, and we find nothing, and we're up to our ears in shit. No, and we find something, we're in shit from our ears down.

We decided to hold fire on a final plan until after the boys had their chat, just in case Blakeson might discover there were more bodies lying around.

"You still a doctor, Jimmy?" Charlie asked him by way of hello.

"Yeah," said Blakeson, "but I'm not giving you anything ..."

"It's not that ... I've got a terrible pain in my back. Any chance you could take a look?"

"Take off your shirt, you drunken bum, and we'll see."

"It's really bad. Did it on the set a couple of weeks ago. Can't remember how. They gave me a whole bunch of horse tablets. But they've all worn off now."

"Yeah, sure. You're still not getting anything... ah, I see what's wrong. You're misaligned. Probably a bad strain. Let me see if I can tweak it straight."

"Must have lifted something wrong ..."

"What were you lifting?"

"I dunno. Some dumb actress no doubt. You gonna come visit me in jail?"

"No way. Hate the places. I'm far too pretty. You'll do just fine in there, though ..."

The two friends laughed easily.

"I'm sorry," said Charlie gently.

"Me too," said Blakeson just as quietly. Then, "She wants to see you, you know ..."

"Who?"

"Sue. She called into the office today when she heard you were supposed to be lying on my operating table. I hadn't seen her since the day you left."

"You're kidding?"

"Nope. Says she never got married ..."

"Neither did I ... how's she looking?"

"Better than you ..."

They laughed again. "Like a million of your money," added Blakeson.

"Has she forgiven me yet …?"

"For what?"

"For killing her off like that. Refusing to write or take her calls. Then blaming her when she tried to pick up with someone else."

"Jesus, man, you were twenty, and she was seventeen. These things happen."

"Yeah, but I cut her dead."

"True – but you were just trying to cope. She knew that then and knows it now … so, do you wanna meet with her?"

"What do *you* think? Might be too late, though."

After a pause, Blakeson spoke again: "I told the cops you would never have killed someone and hid it like that. It's not your style."

"Then why the hell has that dead girl been haunting me every single day for the past week?"

Just then in the little control room, Tommy Bowtie's eyes lit up and he smiled broadly. The lawyer looked directly into the Assistant Commissioner's face and spoke just four words. "I know what happened."

Twenty minutes later, the squad car with the film director inside pulled up at the Embassy back door. I could hear him coming down the hall, demanding to know what in the hell this was about and bitching to the cop that he was going to lodge a complaint with me personally as soon as this was all over. How we'd been friends since kindergarten and talked every day on the phone. If ever an industry bred assholes …

Tommy, Ed and I got him settled in the conference room, gave him a large bourbon to calm him down and then got started.

"Tell us the plot to your new movie," said Ed.

And that, as you guessed, put an end to our story…

It is, of course, a horror flick where our man knocks down and kills a girl during a fog, before burying her in a Dublin park. But the twist – and you'll love this – is that when he goes looking for her body twenty years later, it's gone.

According to the director, Charlie ripped his back lifting a six-stone dummy over a fence about twelve days ago and has been whacked out on under-the-counter ketamine ever since. By Sunday past, he'd resorted to self-medicating as well, and the next thing they knew he was in Pearse Street Garda Station, and they couldn't get anywhere near him. Meanwhile, he was stuck inside, with more drugs in him than Elvis, confessing to his latest movie.

We laughed so hard we nearly called in the Secret Service to have the director shot.

After an hour of assorted explanations and just as many threats, we let everybody go. Blakeson took Charlie off to meet Sue, and the director swanned off to the Clarence Hotel, promising to call me tomorrow.

Ed, Tommy and myself sat and finished the bottle, counting our blessings, until Ellie came in and ordered them home.

She poured herself a small brandy and sat down beside me. "So, a struggling young wannabe becomes famous and ditches his girl. She gets another boy, and he loses his mind with grief. Spends the rest of his life committing slow suicide."

I nodded slowly, fully aware of where this was going.

"She was right there for him, but as soon as he saw the lights he just walked off. Broke her heart and wrecked his own life into the bargain."

"Indeed," I replied, watching her lay it on with a shovel.

"Isn't it terrible what happens when you give up your best friends for fame and fortune?"

"Awful," I agreed.

"God-dammit Dave, are you not getting the point of this at all?" she snapped, suddenly firing up.

So, with that, I put my hand in my pocket and held up the little ring-box.

"Gotcha," I said.

She looked at me in shock, horror and delight, before starting to laugh.

"You sure did, you bastard."

And she snatched the box from my hand.
So be sure and finish off that speech you've been writing for the past thirty-seven years, Pop. You'll finally get to deliver it over here in a month's time.
I love it when I win one.
So long and slán
David

The End

THE CHRISTMAS PRESENT

Author's note: this story was first published by Guildhall Press as a limited-edition novella for Christmas 2016

To the Happy Few

T he retired armed robber Charles 'Getemup' Gormley and his wife Moustache Sally are probably the best couple I know. They are also the longest surviving, if you discount an unfortunate six-week sabbatical a couple of decades back when Sal decides to go full hairy-legged Socialist, and Getemup ups and leaves her for a pretty young hairdresser. That situation, indeed, is made even more complicated by the fact that the pretty young hairdresser is also a pretty young man, which greatly challenges Sal's open-minded thinking. But that is before Harry the Hurler works out the whole melarr is a ruse on Getemup's part to get his wife to meet him halfway and occasionally wash her donkey jacket, and he, that is Harry, reconciles the couple.

Anyhow that is a whole other story entirely and not for today. And all we need to know for now is that Getemup and Sal are in most respects a perfect match. They are both very handsome and considered great catches when they are young. They are bright, they are generous, they are well loved by their friends, and they spend their whole time laughing together. Indeed, they are so perfect a match that as they get older, even their faults chime. For example, today Sal has a voice so loud it can scare the ashes from an urn, while Getemup is about 80 percent deaf because of his first career as lead singer and stringsman with his swing band. Getemup, indeed, is perhaps the only person I know ever to compliment Sal on her karaoke, apart, perhaps, from their next-door neighbour, who will drop off a flagon of Sal's favourite fortified sherry and a box of sheet music any time his mother-in-law is coming to visit.

Sal is also brilliant at handling the bobs and organising the ledgers, which she learns from her days as a manager in her father's bookies. Which is important, as Getemup, while undoubtedly highly talented at gathering in the dollars at their needle-to-an-iPhone cut-price store, will swap these same dollars for a handful of magic beans, or a bet on a football game, unless someone steps in quickly and slaps him on the mouth. Which, of course, Sal, is only too prepared to do.

It is actually in a bookie's shop that Sal and Getemup first meet up, on opposite sides of the counter, about forty years since. And three weeks later, Sal stands up in the witness box and reluctantly confirms that yes, Charles 'Getemup' Gormley is indeed the same guy who waves the plastic gun in her face, before two of her clerks chase him down the street and prise the sixty lousy quid and change out of his broken fingers. Though even the judge, who bangs Getemup away for 18 months, doubts that Getemup rips off his own mask and bounces the door of the getaway car three times off his own knuckles before the gendarmes land on the scene and break it all up.

Contrary to tradition, Getemup is not robbing the shop, as most clientele do, in an attempt to win back his own money, but rather to acquire the down payment on a new black maple jazz guitar for his fellow bandsman Second Best.

Second Best is so named because, while he is not specifically good at anything in particular, he can fill in if you are short of the real deal. Now and again, he will even take over at the mike when Getemup wants to sit out a couple of songs and tell lies to the featherheads making puppy-eyes at him from the front row.

And Second Best's pipes are not bad at all, although he will never make your mother cry, in a good way, like Getemup will, nor is he built like an ad for the gym.

But Second Best is even worse with money than Getemup and never has enough bobs spare to buy a mouth organ from Woolworths never mind a 400-nicker black maple jazz guitar, so he proposes the heist. Second Best unfortunately cannot take part in the robbery himself as he is so well known in the bookies he is regarded by them as a favourite son. Indeed, just like a favourite son, not a week goes by that he does not hand them over his full wage packet and whatever else nearby that is not fastened down. So when he sees Getemup being chased from the shop by his pals the clerks, he legs it from the getaway car and does not draw breath until he is safely 500 miles away in London.

By the time Getemup gets out of jail nine months of good behaviour later, two things are changed. Firstly, he is engaged to Moustache Sally, who deduces, correctly, that he badly needs redeeming and visits him once a fortnight in the civilian wing at HMP Magilligan.

Initially, Sal only calls with Getemup to apologise for his unintentional incarceration and to explain to him that the police's presence is an entire coincidence, as she and her clerks prefer to keep matters in-house. And they will probably not now shoot him as intended.

But Getemup is so tickled by this smart and bossy young visitor, who is also back then very gorgeous, that he bids her stay and talk for the full hour. And, against all the odds, Sal finds herself captivated by this honey-voiced charmer with the Sinatra-blue eyes, laughing loudly when he thanks her troops for restricting all retribution to his strumming hand and not his fret-fingering one. And by the end of that first chat, Sal and Getemup are both starting to realise that, through no design of their own, they are now, and always will be, two halves of the one story. And they are both truly, madly and deeply happy with that.

The other thing that changes while Getemup is inside is that Second Best is now the owner of a maple jazz guitar which, as the maestro Mister Runyon says, is blacker than a yard up a chimney. Second Best is also, more surprisingly, the toast of the West End, and every critic in London is raving about the lilting Irish vocals on his debut swing album. But Getemup is too contented with Sal, and their plans to set up their own market stall, to worry about his old pal's success, no matter how undeserving and uncontactable he is.

The years roll by, and the Getemups find a beautiful little house, where there are no other criminals lowering the tone of the neighbourhood, and raise two beautiful daughters. The couple become the backbone of the Derry middle class, pillars of the civic society. Despite life's slings and arrows, they still love one another, honour one another, and are true to one another. And Getemup always respects and obeys Sal, at least on all those times when she is looking directly at him. And, of course, they remember to laugh together often and always to be kind to one another always.

But then, shortly before their fortieth anniversary, a number of spanners are thrown into the hard drive.

It all kicks off when in the run-up to Christmas, Sally Junior, their youngest, announces she wants to get married to her snot of a fiancé. And she wants to do this someplace far, far away, with warm sand beneath her toes, with a huge crowd of guests in tow, and an archway of roses, and a big basket of doves. Oh, and she wants Daddy to pay for all of it.

Getemup is narked and he voices it to Old Sal. 'We spoil those girls,' he says. 'It is as if they can see directly into our bank balances, work out exactly what we can afford to lose and then double it. Our own wedding breakfast, which is the happiest meal of my life, is eight of us eating homemade stew and wheaten bread over the town in Swankie Frankie's. What is the need for all this fuss?'

What Getemup is not saying is that, while he and Sal are now comfortably off, it is at a cost. They live in the same little house, work seven days a week, rarely take holidays or eat out other than at Frankie's, and drive a cramped mid-range jeep that has a false floor built in to accommodate 400 cartons of imported cigarettes at any given time. Meanwhile, Charlotte and Sal Junior each have their own new sports car and a house in the suburbs. And at least twice a year, they travel to Paris or London or New York to shows like the new one Second Best is about to open in on Broadway. So for the first time in his life, Getemup, who is keen to put any spare bobs towards a brand new jeep with no false bottoms or failing that a new pair of non-leak shoes, is starting to feel hard done by.

But for once, his wife is not on the same page. 'I don't want you getting mean as you get old, Gee,' she says. 'I want to hear you laughing again. I think you forget that it is no bed of roses for anyone in this current cold climate, and that if we can spread a little joy and kindness into anyone else's world, we must do so. Because when all the shouting is done, we are all going to the one place, so it is important that we make the best of the journey. And when we are all dead, that is all that will count on our score-cards. No-one is interested in our final bank tally.'

'Except, of course, our two children,' says Getemup. And they both laugh.

Sal is a shrewd doll and she is skilled at managing Getemup when he is upset, and usually this will be the end of the matter.

But the following morning Getemup's old stand-in Second Best announces in all the newspapers that he will be playing a surprise Christmas Eve concert that very night on Derry's Ebrington Square before he heads off to the Big Apple. And of course the newspapers are billing this event like it is the second coming. But none of them remembers the fact that Getemup is a far better singer than Second Best, nor, moreover, that Second Best is after stealing Getemup's life.

Getemup is so needled that he scrunches up the paper and tosses it into the bin under the shop counter. 'Second Best is an affront,' he says. 'After all this time, and all that happens since, he never once gets in touch. And now he's coming back here to hoover up the entire town's hard-earned Christmas savings at thirty dabs for an open-air seat.'

Sal shakes her head. 'The way I hear it,' she says, 'even if Second Best keeps singing in Carnegie Hall until he's 120, he'll still not have enough money to pay off his three ex-wives, four mortgages and our old friend the taxman. And thirty dabs is not a lot to pay to see a man who is going to be commanding four times that on Broadway next month. His entire fee will just about pay the travel for his backing band. You, on the other hand, owe nothing but this week's football stake and have a hefty pension that will let you retire in just two years time.'

Sal is not being entirely forthcoming in her answer, however. While it is true that Getemup is worth quite a hefty pile, it is not true at all to say that Second Best is never in touch. Indeed, he is in touch with Sal at least once a year since he heads off to London, despite her insistence that he must leave her alone and never contact her again. And the reason she does not want him getting in touch is that Second Best is head over heels in love with her for forty years now, ever since the first minute he claps eyes on her in her father's bookies. Long before Getemup is ever on the scene. Though Sal never breathes a word of this to her husband.

'You can't seriously compare our worlds?' says Getemup. 'His is Vegas with Sinatra, Hawaii with Presley and the White House with Clinton. Mine is the Brandywell for the football, cigarette runs to Dublin with your father and the Lifford Dog Track for our Christmas night out. He gets to pose with Madonna on the red carpet, I get to shampoo the red mat at the door, after the punters drag in their dog-crap. He gets to sing on television for millions, I get to sing along with the radio when no-one's listening.'

'And whose fault is that?' says Sal. She is tired of feeling sorry for Getemup by now. And, as you'll recall she is a lady who can turn quickly. 'You never stop crying about how you are a better act. But the simple truth is you're not. It's easy to be a big fish in a small pool, like you many moons ago, but to make it really big, you need to be special. And I'm sorry to say this, but you need to hear it, maybe Second Best is better than you think...'

She walks over to the counter, picks the paper out of the bin and smooths it out at the double-page spread on the concert. 'Who knows, I might even go over and say hello to him myself tonight,' she says. 'I hear he has quite an eye for the *chicas.* I bet he'll remember me.'

This is a cheap crack, particularly given Getemup's very low opinion of Second Best, and his anger beats his tact in the race for the front door.

'Sadly you are forty years too old for him,' he says to Sal. 'And about sixty pounds too heavy to boot.'

Sal takes a sharp breath. 'You and me and both, Fatso,' she says. 'But at least I still have my hair. And at least I can sing...'

The guns are out from under the table and Getemup is quick to fire back. 'You call what you do singing? You ever wonder why I never change my hearing aid once in twenty years. I would sooner listen to baby pigs being fed through a meat slicer than to that loud mouth of yours. The only place you can sing is in court.'

Sal is mightily offended and gasps loudly to let him know. 'What do you mean by that?'

'I mean that if you can ever keep your trap shut for once, maybe, just maybe, I'll get my shot. Instead of handing it that fancy Dan with the mediocre voice and no shoulders who steals my life.'

Sal has had enough and turns the volume up another notch, which in her case is saying something. 'Dear God, do you ever stop whining? Are you really still blaming me for your long weekend at Magilligan holiday camp? Can I remind you that you are the man waving the gun in the air.'

'–Nine months is jail is no day at the beach.'

'–And there is me believing that you really enjoy being behind a locked door with a few young men...'

'What does that mean?'

'You know well what it means.'

'Yeah, I do go for the manly types all right – as you can tell from your mirror.'

'So that's why you're with me then?'

'No, I'm with you for your father's money. Isn't it obvious?'

'Yeah, and I'm with you because your good-looking friend Second Best runs off to London and leaves an idiot carrying the can.'

But it is too much. And it too true. And Sal knows it.

Geteump lifts the newspaper from her hands and tears it in half. 'I'm going to sort that man out once and for all,' he says. And he storms out the door in the direction of the Jack Kennedy Hotel, to get some fuel in his belly.

'Please don't,' says Sal. But it is too late. And even if Getemup's hearing aid is working, he will never hear her over the raging in his head.

Six hours and much refueling later, Getemup is on his way to Ebrington Square to confront Second Best before the concert. The security men know Getemup well from managing bands about the town, which he does now and again in place of singing ever since the girls come along. And they wave him through their cordon and onto the new pedestrians-only Peace Bridge, which connects the city centre to Ebrington across the river. It is a bitterly cold evening, with frost and snow and such, and the bouncers advise Getemup to be very careful on his way, as they can see he is badly out of practice with the drink.

As he is striding fiercely towards the venue, Getemup is muttering to himself, and to a deity he does not believe in, how much better his life will be if he never lays his eyes on Sal.

'I'll tell you, God,' he says, 'if you can ever do one thing for me, it is this. Take me back to the door of the bookie's shop, shake some sense into me and send Second Best up to the counter instead.'

But as the words are leaving his lips, Getemup slips on a patch of ice, his two feet shoot into the air and he lands bang on his noggin, out for the count. And that is all he remembers.

*

When Getemup wakes up, there is a large crowd of security guards around him on the bridge. And they are all panicking to know if he is okay and blaming one another for not sweeping up the ice.

The back of Getemup's head is thumping but remarkably it is unsplit, so he pulls himself up using the handrail on the bridge, and signals to the men that he is okay. But with that a most sweet-looking red-headed doll, who he can't quite place, pushes through the crowd and begins crying and kissing and hugging him.

'Charles, Charles,' she says, for that is Getemup's given name, 'my poor baby, my poor baby. Are you okay? Will you be able to go on tonight?'

Getemup looks back at the gorillas with the walkie-talkies, who seem to recognise the doll with the American accent, and he tells her he is fine.

'What about your hands?' she asks. 'Will you be able to play? We can probably get a stand-in for the double-bass. Just as long as your voice is okay.'

He looks down at his hands where he admires a pair of fawn sheepskin gloves, which are worth the price of a new bicycle. 'My hands are great,' he says.

'So you can play?' she says, hugging him again. And it looks as though tears are running down her cheeks.

'Yes, I can play,' he says.

With that a big cheer goes up from the security men, and also from the huge crowd that is now gathering behind them. And they quickly form a tunnel to let Getemup, or rather Charlie Gee, as they are all calling him, off the bridge and through to his dressing room at the entrance to Ebrington Square. Though truth be told, he is still not at all sure what the hell is going on.

The next three hours are, without question, the greatest of Charlie Gee's life so far. By the time he hits the stage, there are 12,000 people on the square, and all of them – even the thirty or so men who are there – are madly in love with him.

He performs all his hits for them, plays a few fancy riffs on the old bull fiddle, and gets so many encores that he is out of breath running to the fire-exit and back. He even duets with a few guests, including Camilla, the redhead from the bridge, who he learns from the progamme is the 27-year-old co-star on his new Broadway musical – and clearly has a serious notion on him.

After the show, he stands out on the square signing autographs for all sorts of women who welcome him home, wish him a Merry Christmas and slip him their hotel keys and undergarments.

It is all great fun, perhaps the most fun of his life so far, and Charlie Gee just laps up the adoration and appreciation. After an hour of this, Camilla whispers in his ear that the doctor needs another look at him, and she extricates him back to his dressing room, like only a bossy redheaded women can.

'That is quite a bump you have, Mr Gormley,' says the medic. 'Are you experiencing any discomfort, loss of motion or loss of memory?'

'There's no real pain, Doc,' says Getemup. 'Though the noodle is a little askew. I'm still a little dizzy and the memory is very patchy. The words of the songs are no problem, but I'm having a cursed time with faces and places. It's like I'm missing a big chunk of time - maybe the last forty years.'

The old Doc nods wisely. 'Don't worry. It's just a little amnesia. It should all come back within the next few days.'

Camilla, who is watching all this, hands Getemup a large drink, which he refuses.

'Are you doing that for my benefit?' asks the Doc. 'You're only kidding yourself if you are.'

'No,' says Getemup, 'I really don't want it. What with the dizziness and all, I might get sick.'

The Doc laughs. 'It serves me right for believing what I read. According to the papers, you drink grain alcohol by the rusty bucket. Regardless, leave it out for a few days, if you can. I take it the stuff about the Coke is hokum as well? If there is any truth in it, for God's sake, give it a rest for a week or so too. Coke and bangs on the head are a bad mix. And one more thing...'

'What's that?'

'You're best not travelling for a few days too – the pressure in an airplane isn't recommended after a head injury.'

All of a sudden Camilla is very narked. And she shoots the Doc a look that would torch a medium-sized house. 'We are flying out out tomorrow,' she says. 'We have to be in New York to meet my family on Boxing Day, and then rehearsals for the new show start on New Year's Eve. And that's the end of it.'

The Doc ignores her. 'You're travelling on Christmas Day?' he says to Getemup. 'That's a tough gig. Well, I'm afraid I cannot allow that. I'm grounding you, Charlie, for five days minimum. You can go out on the 29th. I won't clear you until then. You won't get insurance.'

Camilla is about to protest again, when the Doc holds up a single finger to her. 'Do you really want to go down in history as the what's-her-name young wannabe responsible for killing one of the world's greatest ever singers? If not, please stay quiet.'

Camilla's face darkens and she bites back a two-word reply.

Getemup just chuckles good-naturedly. 'It will give me time to get to know Derry again, Cam. Why don't we do another concert on Boxing Night, seeing as we're stuck here? We can do it for free this time, for punters who might not have the bobs. Thirty dabs is a lot to shell out, I hear, on the last day before Christmas. I'll even give you an extra couple of songs. Let you have a solo, maybe?'

Camilla cracks a smile in spite of herself, earning a further smile from the Doc, who is very impressed at how adept Getemup is at handling the ladies.

'I'll get the managers onto it right away,' says Cam. And she sashays rapidly out the door before Charlie changes his mind.

After she leaves, the Doc shakes his head in admiration. 'Charlie,' he says. 'That is the finest-looking young woman you are ever with. And that is saying something. And she is also, if you forgive my pointing it out, a glorious singer – almost in your league. Meanwhile, you yourself, despite a lifetime of epic drinking, have the physique and looks of someone half your age. All things considered, and I say this as a man who is around and about this world a whole lot, you are possibly the luckiest man alive. You have the perfect life. And you are a hell of a nice guy to boot.'

Getemup nods. 'Thank you, Doc. And I have to say I do enjoy my life a lot. Indeed, I cannot imagine how it can be any better. I get to sing, play music and meet people. I still have my hair and my teeth, and the women really same to take a real shine to me, for some reason. Though, strictly between ourselves, Cam may have just a little too much fire under the hood for me. I am looking forward to getting my memory back, so I have something to judge her against, to be sure.'

The Doc laughs again then stands up to go. 'Tell you what, so,' he says. 'I will walk you back over the Peace Bridge to your suite at the Jack Kennedy Hotel, which by the way is where you are staying, and you can tell me what could possibly constitute too much fire in your world. I am a tired old man and could really do with some vicarious living.'

The rest of the night passes without incident. Cam understands perfectly that Charlie is too unwell to let her visit him for cocktails in his suite, as she does most every other night. Though she personally is concerned that it may also be something to do with those two young tramps in the micro-skirts hanging about Charlie's dressing room earlier that evening.

The Doc disappears home after pouring himself a double Jameson from the minibar. Getemup, meantime, takes the Doc's advice and steers away from the Coca-Cola but instead makes himself the nicest cup of tea ever, before falling into the deepest, most restful sleep of his life. Though his dreams, like his memory, are completely black.

When Getemup wakes up on Christmas morning he is happy as a child. The moment his eyes open, a handsome young waiter balancing a four foot square breakfast tray comes into his bedroom, immediately followed by another more homely guy toting two champagne-loaded ice-buckets. Which Getemup waves away.

After he puts paid to the food, which leaves not so much as a bump on his skinny frame, he goes into the anteroom, where there are a bunch of wrapped-up presents and two big sacks of cards waiting for him.

The first waiter, who is still there arranging some cards, says to him: 'Merry Christmas, Mister Gee. How is your head?'

'Not so bad, thank you,' says Getemup. 'Though the memory is still no better. Is there any way you can find me a number for that nice old doctor?'

'No problem, sir,' says the waiter. 'Indeed the last thing Doc Clancy says last night is to be sure to invite you to his house for dinner this evening, as he is aware that you have no family left here.'

'What about Cam?'

The waiter smiles. 'The Doc is some operator,' he says. 'It's all taken care of, sir. We are sorting out a virtual link-up with her family in Brooklyn. We have this new facility where it will be like she is sitting on the opposite side of the table from them. So she will be able to tell them all about how she is now the top-of-the-bill headline act at the big concert on Boxing Day. And she is happy as a kitten in a plate of milk.'

The handsome young waiter disappears to count his tip, leaving Getemup to open his presents and cards. There is a new jazz-bow for his double bass from Cam, for when he is tired of playing pizzicato, a set of pilot's lessons from his tour manager, and a mountain of assorted underwear for him to either wear or sniff. There is also what appears to be a set of electronic cooking scales. 'What a thoughtful gift,' he says to himself. 'I must be a bit of a baker.'

Getemup is truly delighted to find out that he is so well loved, and he resolves to spend the rest of the day writing thank you notes for all the presents and cards.

The last gift he sees is a little square thing that he barely notices at first, as it is so small and wrapped in plain brown paper. But when he opens it, it almost takes his breath away. It is a silver-framed picture of a young Charles Gee and his very first band, playing on the stage of the Embassy Ballroom in the early 1970s. And on a folded-up jotter page, there is a note from someone called Christopher Best, saying he is sorry for all the grief he causes Charlie back in the old days, and maybe they can grab a coffee together when he is next in Derry.

All of a sudden Getemup gets a flash of memory. 'Of course,' he says to himself. 'Old Second Best. The greatest stand-in in the business. I wonder what he's doing now? I must ask the Doc. Maybe I'll even get him up for a song tomorrow night if he's fit.'

Getemup is so deliriously happy that his old friend wants to see him that he gets Reception to patch him through to the Doc directly to find out the lay of the land.

'Oh yes,' says the Doc, 'Second Best is doing very well for himself. From what I read, he has even more money than you do – especially since your last divorce. No, ever since Second Best's time in jail, he always falls on his feet. He is married to a lovely girl, Sally, and the two of them run a big discount store together. It's one of those no receipts, no returns places, where you can pick up just about anything, if you don't need a guarantee or a serial number. Sally does all the ledgers while Second Best charms the customers.'

'Do I know her? This Sally?'

'I doubt it. She has no ear for music at all. You might remember her father though, the old bookie out of Carlow Street?'

Getemup furrows his brow. 'It's starting to come back to me a little. Second Best spends half his days in the bookie's...'

'Not any more. Sally has no time for gamblers.'

'I seem to remember that Second's time in jail has something to do with a bookie's shop too? Am I right?'

'Correct, indeed. An armed robbery. Of Sally of all people. But she is very forgiving. And ever since, she spends her days redeeming and reforming him. And truth is, they are very, very content together, and have two lovely girls. One of them is even going to marry my snot of a nephew next year, God help her.'

'Do you think Second Best will come to the concert and perform a song or two with me?'

'It's possible,' says the Doc. 'But he doesn't really sing anymore, not since the girls. And he doesn't look like much any more either, not that he can hold a candle to you to begin with. But in recent years he's putting on a few in the middle and losing a bunch up top. So I'm not sure he'll be up for it. I'll fill you in on the whole story over dinner. Don't be late. And don't worry about bringing anything.'

The dinner at Doc Clancy's is sublime. Mrs Doc is a tremendous hostess and cook, while their grown-up children are thrilled to have a real life celebrity in their midst, even if he can remember very little about it. Getemup is so pleased to be in such lovely company that he doesn't even think about having a drink, which he is also beginning to realise may be a rare thing for him.

He is eager to hear all about how Second Best turns his life around after robbing Sal. Mrs Doc says, word on the street is that Sally is the real brains behind the robbery at the shop, as she is sweet on Second Best for a long time beforehand and wants to give him the money for a new guitar. Though, that is possibly only a made-up story put about by people who find they cannot exchange their new iPhones at Sal's counter. Not even when they burst into flames in their pockets.

As he is leaving for the hotel again, Getemup turns to the Doc to thank him. 'I am so glad to be at home again,' he says. 'This is, without doubt, my best Christmas ever.'

'That's really hard to credit,' says the Doc. 'You are the most popular bachelor on the planet, the guy that George Clooney wants to be when he grows up. You have the ten most gorgeous women on the planet on speed-dial, and your latest flame is so hot that Hell will never let her in the doors, in case she sets off the smoke alarms. But for all that, you're telling me that turkey and trimmings and no booze in this little north Atlantic backwater is the best Christmas ever?'

'It is. And I am very thankful to you for it. I really feel I don't deserve it. I know that my memory is not good, but I get the feeling that it is a long, long time, since anyone is as kind to me as you are to me today. Unless, perhaps, they are looking for something.'

The Doc laughs. 'Maybe I need to start prescribing amnesia to all my patients.'

Getemup shakes his hand and laughs. 'You could do a whole lot worse.'

Back at the hotel, Cam is having the time of her life with her virtual family and is not in the least annoyed not to be invited over to Charlie's suite for cocktails again. After all, he is five years older than her father and needs his sleep after a big meal. And besides, the handsome young waiter says he will be pleased to demonstrate to her how the gym works if she wants to go for a private workout before her big show. He has his own personal key.

On Boxing Day morning, Getemup is still happy as a clam when he wakes up. Again, he can remember very little from before the fall. But his recall of the events since is crystal clear. And he is very much looking forward to playing another concert at the big square.

Try all he will, however, he cannot track down Second Best, who, it seems, likes to go offline, incommunicado and all quiet over the holidays. Even the Doc, who knows everyone and everything in this town, is unable to help.

Most of the chat on the radio all day is about that night's free gig, so Getemup even rings the station to tell them to announce that he is especially looking forward to hosting all his old Derry band mates at the show, and that they are all under orders not to miss it.

The other news on the radio is that it is going to snow again that evening, and the concert organisers are erecting a giant cloth cover over Ebrington Square to shelter the guests. They are also closing the Peace Bridge to all but the VIPs in case some person might slip and bang their head on the ground like Getemup. Except maybe this person will not have either Getemup's money or decency and will sue the organisers for every penny they own.

Getemup spends the day getting a tour of the town from Doc Clancy, who shows him everything from the site of Saint Columb's sixth-century monastery to the spanking new inner-city park opposite the cathedral. Afterwards, they defrost in the Jack Kennedy over a cup of hot chocolate, and an Irish coffee for Doc, while Doc assures Getemup that all will be fine with his noggin in a few weeks tops.

'But what will happen then?' says Getemup. 'Everything I'm reading about myself in the newspapers, and hearing about myself on the television, makes me think I am better off not knowing who I really am at all. I certainly don't want to go back to being that guy. Because between you and me, he sounds like quite an ass. I love my life now. I am never happier than when I am singing. But besides my memory, I feel like I am missing a big part of myself. I have no-one to celebrate it all with, no-one to laugh with and no-one to share my stories with.'

The Doc, who is a wise old bird and well aware that Camilla is only there to scratch an itch, nods. 'I am not sure anyone gets to have it all, Charlie. But the smartest people I know are those who are happy with what they have. I will never have a villa in Tuscany or a private plane like you, but what I do have is a beautiful wife, a lovely home, three well-fed children and a small handful of friends who will drive me home if I am one over the eight. In short, I have people in my life I can complain to when I have a crappy day. And they will listen to me, not for my money, but because I will then listen to them when it is their turn to be grumpy. And at the end of the day, that is all than any one man really needs.'

Getemup's second Ebrington concert, according to both himself and the critics, is his finest hour yet. His voice is golden, his pacing is flawless and his string-playing is immaculate. Add to that the full moon shining on the river, and the snow falling lightly on the stage, and it is as if the heavens themselves are conspiring to make the night just perfect. There are smiles on every face, and there are tears on every cheek, even on the hardest of hard men.

Camilla, too, is thrilled to score a standing ovation of her own, while the crowd is totally charmed when Getemup's old band, The Gee Strings, join him at the end of the night for his fifth and final encore. Even the Mayor gets in on the act, coming up to the stage at the end to thank Getemup for staging the concert and handing him a ceremonial Key to the City for his kindness. Indeed, the only minor fly in the Christmas custard is that there is no sign of Second Best.

Despite the marvelous reception, Getemup is a little low as he changes into his duds in the dressing room afterwards. He decides to skip the backstage party and head back to the hotel for a cup of that terrific tea.

He tips his minder the nod not to let anyone come after him and sets off across the square to the Peace Bridge, which is closed to all but the special guests. It is getting very cold so he sets off at quite a pace to warm himself up.

Getemup is about halfway across the bridge and motoring full pelt when he sees three women and a man hurrying madly back towards Ebrington Square. Indeed, they almost pile into each other, they are all going so hard. But just as they are passing, the man from the group looks back to Getemup and shouts one word: 'Charlie.'

And who is it but a much older version of Getemup's old friend Second Best.

'My God, it is you Chris,' says Getemup, using Second's proper name. 'It is so good to see you. Why are you so late? I'm trying since yesterday to track you down.'

A serene-looking older woman, with a stunning smile and piercing green eyes, hits Second Best a friendly slap as if to say You Big Idiot. 'I'm after dragging him the whole way here from Daddy's little cabin in Donegal,' she says. 'He isn't for coming at all - says you'll never remember him. These are our two daughters, by the way. But I warn you, stay away from them or I will bust you.'

They all laugh at that, and the grey-haired woman, who is about four stone to the good of Getemup and has a very strong voice, sticks out her hand to introduce herself. 'I'm Sally,' she says. 'But

Second Best always calls me Moustache Sally on account of the fact that I am not much of a singer and am renowned for massacring the old Wilson Pickett song on karaoke night.'

Second Best grins apologetically, and at the back of his mind Getemup seems to remember making a similar joke many years before.

'I hear you have amnesia,' says Second Best. 'I hope this means you might forget me causing you all that bother with that robbery mess. I'm responsible for you nearly missing your big chance, when the police won't release our gear because of my thieving and all. Thank God for Doc Clancy and his connections.

'It does not seem to be much of a mess any more,' says Getemup. And he points at the massive stage back over on the square. 'And besides, I am so pleased to see you, Christopher. You look so well.'

This last statement is a bit of a lie, as Second Best is presently fat, bald and dressed like Getemup's grandfather.

'I don't gamble any more,' says Second Best with a proud smile. 'I don't need to, now that I have myself a sure thing.'

And with that, Second Best's wife of forty years leans into him and hugs him with real pleasure. It is so natural and intimate a gesture, and yet childlike in its innocence, that Getemup feels his heart starting to break and his eyes starting to well up. Sally is, without question, the most enchanting person that Getemup remembers meeting in any part of his life. A genuine angel. And Second Best seems just so pleased and so appreciative to have her.

For some unknown reason, Getemup finds himself overwhelmed by the woman's presence. There is a force radiating from her, a grace, that he knows should be in his own life. She has a contentment that he desperately wants to understand, a story that he needs to hear. He just wants to stand on the bridge all night, to listen to her, to talk to her and maybe she will hug him, just once, like she hugs Second Best.

But equally, he knows that that is all plain nuts and that he must get off the bridge immediately to the safety of his hotel.

'Excuse me,' he says to the group. 'I'm coming over a little unwell.

It must be a side effect from the fall the other day. The Doc says I have to take it easy.'

The Second Best family look at one another blankly without saying a word.

'No, really,' says Getemup. 'I don't drink anymore. Or do anything else. And there's no-one waiting for me. It's only me. It's just that I'm feeling a little off. Maybe tomorrow…'

And with that Getemup turns and hurries off towards the cityside of the river leaving a small row of broken faces behind him. But he is barely ten feet from the group, when he slips on a patch of ice, his two feet shoot into the air and he lands bang on his noggin, out for the count. And that is all he remembers.

When Getemup wakes up, there is a large crowd of security guards around him on the bridge. And they are all panicking to know if he is okay and blaming one another for not sweeping up the ice.

The back of Getemup's head is thumping but remarkably it is unsplit, so he pulls himself up using the handrail on the bridge, and signals to the men that he is okay. But with that the grey-haired dame pushes her way through the small crowd and begins hugging him and kissing him.

'Charles, Charles,' she says, for that is Getemup's given name, 'my poor baby, my poor baby. Are you okay? Are you okay? Will you be able to go on tonight?'

Getemup is so shaken he does not know what day it is. And when this beautiful lady starts to hug him, he suddenly starts to cry. He feels so empty that he does not have anyone in his own life like this incredible woman. He is completely engulfed by sadness and consumed with loneliness. But then as he listens to the voice saying 'My poor Charles' over and over again, and feels the tears running down her cheeks too, he realises that this woman is none other than his own wife Sally, and he starts to cry all over again. He finds himself crying with relief, joy and then finally with sheer gratitude. And for the first time in his life he is truly aware at how happy he is.

'I am so sorry,' he says, wiping his nose. 'I'm so, so sorry, Sally. I am such an idiot. What the hell am I thinking, drinking whiskey like that?'

Sal kisses him on the cheek and shakes her head. 'No,' she says. 'It is not you. And while I am usually slow to concede that you can be right about anything, this time you have a point. Second Best is being a real pill not inviting you to this concert. So, he and I meet up for long hard heart-to-heart this afternoon, and I put him right on a few things. He is now agreed that you and The Gee Strings will be joining him on stage for his finale. He is even going to let you have the lead vocals for one song – though not while the TV cameras are running in case you make him look bad.'

Getemup looks back at the gorillas with the walkie-talkies, who are clearing a path to let through an oversized ventriloquist's dummy in a toupee and one-thousand-dollar shoes. He looks exactly like a fifty-nine-year-old version of Getemup's old stand-in Second Best, which of course he is.

Second Best motions to shake Getemup's hand but, as he shoots out his hand, he changes his mind and the two men share a massive bearhug instead. 'You look great, Charlie,' says Second Best. 'So do you, Chris,' says Getemup.

They break their clinch and stand back to admire one another. 'You win,' says Getemup. 'You have more teeth.'

They laugh again.

'I owe you my life,' says Second Best. 'I am so ashamed that I can barely look you in the eye.'

'You owe me nothing,' says Getemup. He squeezes Sally again, and is rewarded with a lovely smile right into his face. 'I do okay. More than okay, actually.'

'Thank you for the gift, by the way,' says Second Best. 'It is very thoughtful of you to frame that old picture of us from the Embassy and send it to my hotel room.'

Getemup hasn't a clue what Second is talking about. But then Sal hits him a sharp nudge so he knows to play along. 'Don't mention it,' he says. 'And thank you in turn for inviting us here tonight.'

'How's your voice?' asks Second.

Getemup shrugs. 'Still better than yours. In fact, I am pretty sure I will blow you off the stage tonight and then sweep your dust into the river.'

Second Best winces at the joke, but only because he knows there is a large element of truth in it. 'Look, Charlie, I'm looking for an orchestral arranger for the new show in New York. Big money. Big, big money in fact. And a bit of stage time to boot. Is there any chance you would consider it.'

Getemup smiles thank you at his friend, then slowly shakes his head no.

'My life is here,' he says. 'And it is wonderful.'

'Yes it is,' says Second Best. 'And you deserve it. Ever since the day and hour I know you, you are always at the right end of the deal.'

'You are right,' says Getemup, 'but sometimes it takes a serious bang on the head to make me remember that.'

And with that, he gives Sal one more big hug, punches his friend on the shoulder and the trio make their way through the tunnel of guards and towards Ebrington Square.

THE END

ABOUT THE AUTHOR

Garbhan Downey

Lifelong Derry native Downey is a writer, editor, broadcaster and publisher.

His first collection of short stories, Off Broadway, published by Guildhall Press (2005), was widely acclaimed, with the Irish News commenting: 'Downey has constructed a world of rogues and crooks that Dickens would have been proud to have created.'

His novels include Once Upon A Time in the North West (2015), War of the Blue Roses (2009) and Running Mates (2007).

Downey founded Colmcille Press in 2019. He lives in Derry with his wife Úna, and they have two children, Fiachra and Brónagh.

Printed in Great Britain
by Amazon